Roald Dahl
Graham Greene
Art Buchwald
Guy de Maupassant
P G Wodehouse
Jack London
D H Lawrence
Marina Mizzau
Vladimir Korolenko
James Thurber
Edgar Allan Poe
Ivan Bunin
nen Leacock
Saki

A Shocking Accident

Stories with a Sting in the Tail

*Edited by Sara Corrin
and co-edited by Eve Corrin*

WALKER BOOKS
AND SUBSIDIARIES
LONDON · BOSTON · SYDNEY

The editor and publisher gratefully acknowledge the permission to use the following material:

"A Shocking Accident", from *The Collected Stories*, Graham Greene, published by
William Heinemann Ltd. Reproduced by permission of David Higham Associates Limited.

"The Necklace", Guy de Maupassant, from *French Stories of the Nineteenth and Twentieth Centuries*,
ed. Frederick Charles Green, published by Dent in the Everyman Library.

"The Fiery Wooing of Mordred", from *Week-End Wodehouse*, P G Wodehouse, published
by Hutchinson. Used by permission of The Random House Group Limited.

"How Un-American Can You Get?", from *Have I Ever Lied to You?*, Art Buchwald.
© 1968 Art Buchwald. Used by permission of G P Putnam's Sons, a division of
Penguin Putnam Inc. for the Philippine Islands.

"At the Airport", Marina Mizzau, from *Italian Women Writing*, ed. Sharon Wood, published
by Manchester University Press. Translated by Tom Errera-Corrin. Used by permission.

"The Night the Bed Fell", from *My Life and Hard Times*, James Thurber.
© 1933, 1961 James Thurber. Reprinted by arrangement with Rosemary Thurber
and The Barbara Hogenson Agency. All rights reserved.

"Roosya", from *The Gentleman from San Francisco*, Ivan Bunin, published by Hogarth Press.
Used by permission of The Random House Group Limited.

"Borrowing a Match", Stephen Leacock, from *Laugh and Learn: Humorous American Short Stories*,
ed. Mira Felder, published by Addison Wesley Longman.
Reprinted by permission of Pearson Education Inc.

"Lamb to the Slaughter", from *Collected Short Stories of Roald Dahl*, published by Penguin.
Reproduced by permission of David Higham Associates Limited.

Every effort has been made to secure permission for the use of copyrighted material.
If notified of any error or omission, the editor and publisher will gladly make the necessary
correction in future printings.

First published 2003 by Walker Books Ltd
87 Vauxhall Walk, London SE11 5HJ

2 4 6 8 10 9 7 5 3 1

Anthology © 2003 Sara Corrin
Cover illustration © 2003 Sara Fanelli

This book has been typeset in Weiss and Gill Sans Bold Extra Condensed

Printed in Great Britain by Cox & Wyman Ltd, Reading, Berkshire

British Library Cataloguing in Publication Data:
a catalogue record for this book is
available from the British Library

ISBN 0-7445-8641-0

Contents

To Tom, Eve and Julia
with all my love

*Sara would like to thank her younger daughter, Julia,
for her unstinting support and advice throughout; her grandson,
Tom, for his translation of "At the Airport" and his warm support;
and not least Averil for her constant help and inspiration.*

SARA CORRIN is well known for the distinguished and popular story collections that she and her late husband, Stephen, anthologized for children, including a series of age-graded collections ranging from *Stories for Under-Fives* to *Stories for Tens and Over*. Sara says her greatest joy is sharing stories with children – as a teacher she became known as the Storyteller, and pupils would come back years after they had left school to recall the tales they had enjoyed in her classes. In her position as Senior Lecturer in Education at a college of education in Hertfordshire, she made children's responses to literature one of her main studies. After her retirement, Sara's storytelling took her to America, Holland and all over Great Britain. Sara has two daughters, Eve and Julia, and a grandson, Tom. Sara lives in London.

Introduction

Stories with a Sting in the Tail

Oscar Wilde, in his story "The Devoted Friend", has a bird discussing friendship with a water rat. "While we're on the subject of friendship," says the bird, "I'll tell you a story."

"Is it about me?" asks the water rat. "If so I'll listen, for I'm mighty fond of fiction."

Aren't we all! We love listening to stories and often find something of ourselves within them. The stories in this collection include a range of human experiences and emotions, from the familiar to the exotic, the humorous to the poignant. They all have a certain twist or quirkiness to them, shocking and disturbing in some, in others light and playful.

Several of the darker stories deal with what lurks beneath conventional surfaces. Maupassant's classic "The Necklace" illustrates the pitfalls of pride. A sinister note is struck in "Lamb to the Slaughter" and "The Tell-Tale Heart", both of which reveal the fathomless depths of the human psyche. Jack London's powerful but bleak study of a man and his dog in extreme circumstances – "To Build a Fire" – is a tour de force of sustained intensity that reminds us of the frailty of the human condition. "The Rocking-Horse Winner" and "Sredni Vashtar" are disturbing studies of unhappy, marginalized children in the care of adults who do not understand their intense inner worlds. "Children of the Vaults" also embraces this theme. This poignant story touches on the problems of poverty, homelessness and loss. But above all it is about the redemptive power of love.

Several of the stories take a light-hearted look at the way people behave, including the irony of "How Un-American Can You Get?", the comical mental convolutions in "At the Airport" and the preposterous behaviour of the characters in "Borrowing a Match". Thurber's farce "The Night the Bed Fell" shows us the unexpected — but hilarious — consequences of jumping to conclusions without knowing the whole story.

The collection also includes three love stories: the heart-warming tragicomedy "A Shocking Accident", P G Wodehouse's humorous "The Fiery Wooing of Mordred", and "Roosya" with its strange, sensuous beauty.

Where novels are land masses or continents, short stories are islands: they are small, self-contained worlds that allow you to glimpse the essence of each writer. We hope you will enjoy island-hopping!

Sara and Eve Corrin

A Shocking Accident

Graham Greene

Jerome was called into his housemaster's room in the break between the second and the third class on a Thursday morning. He had no fear of trouble, for he was a warden – the name that the proprietor and headmaster of a rather expensive preparatory school had chosen to give to approved, reliable boys in the lower forms (from a warden one became a guardian and finally before leaving, it was hoped for Marlborough or Rugby, a crusader). The housemaster, Mr Wordsworth, sat behind his desk with an appearance of perplexity and apprehension. Jerome had the odd impression when he entered that he was a cause of fear.

"Sit down, Jerome," Mr Wordsworth said. "All going well with the trigonometry?"

"Yes, sir."

"I've had a telephone call, Jerome. From your aunt. I'm afraid I have bad news for you."

"Yes, sir?"

"Your father has had an accident."

"Oh."

Mr Wordsworth looked at him with some surprise. "A serious accident."

"Yes, sir?"

Jerome worshipped his father: the verb is exact. As man re-creates God, so Jerome re-created his father – from a restless widowed author into a mysterious adventurer who travelled in far places – Nice, Beirut, Majorca, even the Canaries. The time had arrived about his eighth birthday when Jerome believed that his father either "ran guns" or was a member of the British Secret Service. Now it occurred to him that his father might have been wounded in "a hail of machine-gun bullets".

Mr Wordsworth played with the ruler on his desk. He seemed at a loss how to continue. He said, "You know your father was in Naples?"

"Yes, sir."

"Your aunt heard from the hospital today."

"Oh."

Mr Wordsworth said with desperation, "It was a street accident."

"Yes, sir?" It seemed quite likely to Jerome that they would call it a street accident. The police of course had fired first; his father would not take human life except as a last resort.

"I'm afraid your father was very seriously hurt indeed."

"Oh."

"In fact, Jerome, he died yesterday. Quite without pain."

"Did they shoot him through the heart?"

"I beg your pardon. What did you say, Jerome?"

"Did they shoot him through the heart?"

"Nobody shot him, Jerome. A pig fell on him." An inexplicable convulsion took place in the nerves of Mr

Wordsworth's face; it really looked for a moment as though he were going to laugh. He closed his eyes, composed his features and said rapidly as though it were necessary to expel the story as rapidly as possible. "Your father was walking along a street in Naples when a pig fell on him. A shocking accident. Apparently in the poorer quarters of Naples they keep pigs on their balconies. This one was on the fifth floor. It had grown too fat. The balcony broke. The pig fell on your father."

Mr Wordsworth left his desk rapidly and went to the window, turning his back on Jerome. He shook a little with emotion.

Jerome said, "What happened to the pig?"

This was not callousness on the part of Jerome, as it was interpreted by Mr Wordsworth to his colleagues (he even discussed with them whether, perhaps, Jerome was yet fitted to be a warden). Jerome was only attempting to visualize the strange scene to get the details right. Nor was Jerome a boy who cried; he was a boy who brooded, and it never occurred to him at his preparatory school that the circumstances of his father's death were comic — they were still part of the mystery of life. It was later, in his first term at his public school, when he told the story to his best friend, that he began to realize how it affected others. Naturally after that disclosure he was known, rather unreasonably, as Pig.

Unfortunately his aunt had no sense of humour. There was an enlarged snapshot of his father on the piano; a large sad man in an unsuitable dark suit posed in Capri with an umbrella (to guard him against sunstroke), the Faraglione rocks forming the background. By the age of sixteen Jerome was well aware that the portrait looked more like the author of *Sunshine and Shade* and *Rambles in the Balearics* than an agent of the Secret Service. All the same he loved the memory of his father: he still possessed an album fitted with picture-postcards (the stamps had been soaked off long ago for his other collection), and it pained him when his aunt embarked with strangers on the story of his father's death.

"A shocking accident," she would begin, and the stranger would compose his or her features into the correct shape for interest and commiseration. Both reactions, of course, were false, but it was terrible for Jerome to see how suddenly, midway in her rambling discourse, the interest would become genuine. "I can't think how such things can be allowed in a civilized country," his aunt would say. "I suppose one has to regard Italy as civilized. One is prepared for all kinds of things abroad, of course, and my brother was a great traveller. He always carried a water-filter with him. It was far less expensive, you know, than buying all those bottles of mineral water. My brother always said that his filter paid for his dinner wine. You can see from that what a careful man he was, but who could possibly have expected when he was walking along the Via Dottore Manuele Panucci on his way to the Hydrographic Museum that a pig would fall on him?" That was the moment when the interest became genuine.

Jerome's father had not been a very distinguished writer, but the time always seems to come, after an author's death, when somebody thinks it worth his while to write a letter to the *Times Literary Supplement* announcing the preparation of a biography and asking to see any letters or documents or receive any anecdotes from friends of the dead man. Most of the biographies, of course, never appear – one wonders whether the whole thing may not be an obscure form of blackmail and whether many a potential writer of a biography or thesis finds the means in this way to finish his education at Kansas or Nottingham. Jerome, however, as a chartered accountant, lived far from the literary world. He did not realize how small the menace really was, or that the danger period for someone of his father's obscurity had long passed. Sometimes he rehearsed the method of recounting his father's death so as to reduce the comic element to its smallest dimensions – it would be of no use to refuse information, for in that case the biographer would undoubtedly visit his aunt who was living to a great old age with no sign of flagging.

It seemed to Jerome that there were two possible methods – the first led gently up to the accident, so that by the time it was described the listener was so well prepared that the death came really as an anticlimax. The chief danger of laughter in such a story was always surprise. When he rehearsed this method Jerome began boringly enough.

"You know Naples and those high tenement buildings? Somebody once told me that the Neapolitan always feels at home in New York just as the man from Turin feels at home in London because the river runs in much the same way in both cities. Where was I? Oh, yes. Naples, of course. You'd be surprised in the poorer quarters what things they keep on the balconies of those sky-scraping tenements – not washing, you know, or bedding, but things like livestock, chickens or even pigs. Of course the pigs get no exercise whatever and fatten all the quicker." He could imagine how his hearer's eyes would have glazed by this time. "I've no idea, have you, how heavy a pig can be, but these old buildings are all badly in need of repair. A balcony on the fifth floor gave way under one of those pigs. It struck the third floor balcony on its way down and sort of ricochetted into the street. My father was on the way to the Hydrographic Museum when the pig hit him. Coming from that height and that angle it broke his neck." This was really a masterly attempt to make an intrinsically interesting subject boring.

The other method Jerome rehearsed had the virtue of brevity.

"My father was killed by a pig."

"Really? In India?"

"No, in Italy."

"How interesting. I never realized there was pig-sticking in Italy. Was your father keen on polo?"

In course of time, neither too early nor too late, rather as though, in his capacity as a chartered accountant, Jerome had studied the statistics and taken the average, he became engaged to be married: to a pleasant fresh-faced girl of twenty-five whose father was a doctor in Pinner. Her name was Sally, her favourite author was still Hugh Walpole, and she had adored babies ever since she had been given a doll at the age of five which moved its eyes and made water. Their relationship was contented rather than exciting, as became the love affair of a chartered accountant; it would never have done if it had interfered with the figures.

One thought worried Jerome, however. Now that within a year he might himself become a father, his love for the dead man increased; he realized what affection had gone into the picture-postcards. He felt a longing to protect his memory, and uncertain whether this quiet love of his would survive if Sally were so insensitive as to laugh when she heard the story of his father's death. Inevitably she would hear it when Jerome brought her to dinner with his aunt. Several times he tried to tell her himself, as she was naturally anxious to know all she could that concerned him.

"You were very small when your father died?"

"Just nine."

"Poor little boy," she said.

"I was at school. They broke the news to me."

"Did you take it very hard?"

"I can't remember."

"You never told me how it happened."

"It was very sudden. A street accident."

"You'll never drive fast, will you, Jemmy?" (She had begun to call him "Jemmy".) It was too late then to try the second method – the one he thought of as the pig-sticking one.

They were going to marry quietly in a registry office and have their honeymoon at Torquay. He avoided taking her to see his aunt until a week before the wedding, but then the night came, and he could not have told himself whether his apprehension was more for his father's memory or the security of his own love.

The moment came all too soon. "Is that Jemmy's father?" Sally asked, picking up the portrait of the man with the umbrella.

"Yes, dear. How did you guess?"

"He has Jemmy's eyes and brow, hasn't he?"

"Has Jerome lent you his books?"

"No."

"I will give you a set for your wedding. He wrote so tenderly about his travels. My own favourite is *Nooks and Crannies*. He would have had a great future. It made that shocking accident all the worse."

"Yes?"

Jerome longed to leave the room and not see that loved face crinkle with irresistible amusement.

"I had so many letters from his readers after the pig fell on him." She had never been so abrupt before.

And then the miracle happened. Sally did not laugh. Sally sat with open eyes of horror while his aunt told her the story, and at the end, "How horrible," Sally said. "It makes you think, doesn't it? Happening like that. Out of a clear sky."

Jerome's heart sang with joy. It was as though she had appeased his fear for ever. In the taxi going home he kissed her with more passion than he had ever shown and she returned it. There were babies in her pale blue pupils, babies that rolled their eyes and made water.

"A week today," Jerome said, and she squeezed his hand. "Penny for your thoughts, my darling."

"I was wondering," Sally said, "what happened to the poor pig?"

"They almost certainly had it for dinner," Jerome said happily and kissed the dear child again.

The Necklace

Guy de Maupassant

She was one of those pretty, charming girls, born, as if by a mistake of destiny, into a family of clerks. She had no dowry, no expectations, no means of being known, understood, loved, wedded by a rich, distinguished man; and she let herself be married to a petty clerk at the Ministry of Education.

She was simply dressed, not being able to dress richly; but unhappy, like a woman out of her class; for women have no caste or race, their beauty, their grace and their charm serve them for good birth and family. Their native sensitiveness, their instinct for elegance, their subtlety of mind are their only hierarchy, and make girls of the people the equals of the greatest ladies.

She suffered ceaselessly, feeling herself born for every delicacy and every luxury. She suffered from the poverty of her home, from the wretched look of the walls, from the worn-out seats, from the ugliness of the materials. All these things, which another woman of her class would not even have noticed, tortured and distressed her. The sight of the little Breton girl who did her simple housework for her, roused in her desolating regrets and distracted dreams. She dreamed of quiet ante-chambers, padded with oriental hangings, lit by bronze candelabras, and of two tall footmen in knee-breeches, who slept in the wide armchairs in the heavy heat of a hot-air stove. She dreamed of big reception-rooms, draped in silks of old time, of fine furniture set out with priceless knick-knacks, and of little dainty drawing-rooms, perfumed, made for five o'clock chats with one's most intimate friends, men known and sought after, whose attentions all the women envied and desired.

When she sat down for dinner, before the round table, covered with a three-days-old tablecloth, opposite her husband who took the lid off the soup tureen, and declared with an air of enchantment: "Ah! the good old boiled beef and carrots! I don't know anything better than that!" she was dreaming of elegant dinners, of glittering plate, of tapestries that peopled the walls with figures of the days of old and with strange birds amidst a fairy forest: she was dreaming of exquisite food served in marvellous dishes, of whispered compliments listened to with a sphinx-like smile, the while she ate the pink flesh of a trout, or the wings of a grouse.

She had no fine dresses, no jewels, nothing. And she loved those things only, she felt herself made for them. She would have liked so much to please, to be envied, to be seductive and exquisite.

She had a rich woman friend, a comrade of convent days, whom she didn't want to go and see, she suffered so much in coming back. And she would weep for whole days, from sorrow, from regret, from despair, and from wretchedness.

*   *   *

Now, one evening, her husband came in proudly, and holding in his hand a large envelope.

"Here," he said, "there's something for you."

She tore open the paper quickly and brought out a printed card which bore these words:

"The Minister of Education and Madame Georges Ramponneau request Monsieur and Madame Loisel to do them the honour of coming to spend the evening at the Ministry, on Monday, the 18th January."

Instead of being delighted, as her husband had hoped, she threw the invitation peevishly on the table, murmuring:

"What do you expect me to do with that?"

"But, my dear, I thought you'd be glad. You never go out, and this is an opportunity, a fine one. I've had no end of trouble to get it. Everybody wants one: it is very exclusive, and not many invitations are given to the clerks. You'll see all the people who hold office there."

She looked at him angrily, and she declared impatiently:

"What do you expect me to put on to go there?"

He hadn't thought of that; he stammered:

"But the dress you go to the theatre in. I think that's a very nice one—"

He stopped speaking, stupefied, aghast, seeing that his wife was crying. Two big tears slowly descended from the corners of her eyes to the corners of her mouth; he faltered:

"What's the matter? What's the matter?"

But with a violent effort, she had subdued her distress, and she answered in a calm voice, drying her wet cheeks:

"Nothing. Only I have no dress, and consequently I can't

go to this reception. Give your card to one of your colleagues whose wife is better got up than I am."

He was in despair. He tried again:

"See here, Mathilde. How much would it cost to get a suitable dress, which you could use again on other occasions, something very simple?"

She reflected a few seconds, reckoning up the cost, and thinking as well of a sum that she could ask for without an immediate refusal and a frightened exclamation from the thrifty clerk.

"I don't know just exactly, but it seems to me that with four hundred francs I could do it."

He grew rather pale, for he was laying aside just that sum to buy a gun and treat himself to hunting parties, next summer, on the plains of Nanterre, with some friends who were going to shoot at larks down there, on Sundays.

He said all the same:

"All right. I'll give you four hundred francs. But try to have a handsome dress."

The day of the reception was drawing near, and Madame Loisel seemed sad, uneasy, anxious. All the same her dress was ready. Her husband said to her one evening:

"What's the matter? see here, you've been in a funny state for three days."

And she answered:

"I'm vexed at not having some jewels, not a single stone, nothing to put on me. I shall look dreadfully poverty-stricken. I'd almost rather not go to this affair."

He took her up:

"You can wear real flowers. It's very fashionable this season. For ten francs you can have two or three magnificent roses."

She was not convinced.

"No. There's nothing more humiliating than to look poor among rich women."

But her husband cried out:

"How silly you are! Go and find your friend, Madame Forestier, and ask her to lend you some jewels. You're friendly enough with her to do that."

She uttered a joyous cry.

"That's true. I hadn't thought of that."

The next day she went to her friend, and told her her trouble. Madame Forestier went to her glass-fronted wardrobe, took a large jewel box, brought it over, opened it, and said to Madame Loisel:

"Choose for yourself, my dear."

She saw first bracelets, then a string of pearls, then a Venetian cross, gold, and precious stones, admirably worked. She tried on the ornaments before the mirror, hesitated, could not decide to leave them, to give them up. She asked constantly:

"Have you nothing else?"

"Yes. Look; I don't know what might please you."

Suddenly she discovered, in a black satin box, a superb string of diamonds. And her heart began to beat with an unmeasured desire. Her hands trembled as she took it up. She fastened it round her throat, on her high dress, and stood in ecstasy before her reflection.

Then she asked, hesitating, full of anguish:

"Could you lend me this, nothing but this?"

"Yes, certainly."

She flung her arms round her friend's neck, kissed her with abandon, then fled with her treasure.

The day of the reception arrived. Madame Loisel had a triumph. She was prettier than all the other ladies, elegant, gracious, smiling, and mad with joy. All the men were looking at her, asking her name, seeking to be introduced to her. All the attachés of the Ministry were wanting to waltz with her. The Minister noticed her.

She danced madly, with abandon, drunk with pleasure, thinking of nothing, in the triumph of her beauty, in the glory of her success, in a sort of cloud of happiness, made up of all those compliments, all this admiration, all those awakened desires, this victory so complete, and so sweet to a woman's heart.

She left about four o'clock in the morning. Her husband, since midnight, had been asleep in a little deserted room with three other men whose wives were having a good time.

He threw on her shoulders the garments he had brought for going home, modest garments of every day, whose poverty contrasted horribly with the elegance of her ball dress. She felt it, and wanted to flee, so as not to be seen by the other women who were wrapping themselves in rich furs.

Loisel detained her.

"Wait a bit. You'll catch a cold outside. I'm going to call a cab."

But she didn't listen to him, and quickly ran down the staircase. When they were in the street, they couldn't find a cab: and they began to look for one, shouting after the cab-drivers that they saw passing in the distance.

They went down towards the Seine, desperate, shivering. Finally they found on the quay, one of those old night-walking broughams that are not seen in Paris except when night falls, as if they had been ashamed of their wretched appearance during the day.

It took them to their door, Rue des Martyrs, and they climbed wearily up to their flat. It was all over, for her. And he was thinking that he had to be at the Ministry at ten o'clock.

She took off the garments in which she had wrapped her shoulders, before the mirror, so that she could see herself once again in her glory. But suddenly she cried out. She had no longer her string of diamonds round her neck.

Her husband, already half undressed, asked:

"What's the matter with you?"

She turned to him, distractedly.

"I have— I have— I have not got Madame Forestier's necklace."

He sat up, aghast.

"What? How? It isn't possible."

And they looked in the folds of her dress, in the folds of her coat, in the pockets, everywhere. They did not find it.

He asked:

"Are you sure you had it still when you left the ball?"

"Yes. I touched it in the vestibule of the Ministry."

"But if you had lost it in the street, we should have heard it fall. It must be in the cab."

"Yes. That's likely. Did you take the number?"

"No. And you, didn't you notice it?"

"No."

They looked at one another, overwhelmed. Finally Loisel put on his clothes again.

"I am going," he said, "to retrace all the walk we did on foot, to see if I shall not find it."

And he went out. She stayed in her evening dress, without strength to go to bed, collapsed in a chair, without fire, without thought.

Her husband came in about seven o'clock. He had found nothing.

He went to the police office, to the newspapers to offer a reward, to the companies that let out cabs for hire, everywhere, in short, where a glimmer of hope attracted him.

She waited all day, in the same state of distraction before this frightful disaster.

Loisel returned in the evening, his cheeks hollowed, pale; he had discovered nothing.

"You must," he said, "write to your friend that you have broken the clasp of her diamonds, and that you are having it repaired. That will give us time to turn round."

She wrote, to his dictation.

At the end of a week they had lost all hope. And Loisel, five years older, declared:

"We must make arrangements to replace this jewellery."

They took, next day, the box in which it had been contained, and went to the jeweller whose name was inside. He consulted his books:

"It is not I, madame, who sold this necklace: I can only have supplied the case."

Then they went from jeweller to jeweller, seeking a necklace like the other, searching their memories, ill, both of them, with grief and anguish.

They found in a shop in the Palais-Royal, a string of diamonds that seemed to them exactly like the one they were looking for. It was worth forty thousand francs. They would let them have it for thirty-six thousand.

They begged the jeweller not to sell it for three days. And they made an arrangement that it would be taken back at thirty-four thousand francs if the first string was found before the end of February.

Loisel possessed eighteen thousand francs that his father had left him. He would borrow the rest.

He borrowed, asking a thousand francs from one man, five hundred from another, a hundred francs here, sixty there. He gave promissory notes, made ruinous engagements, had business with usurers, with all the race of money-lenders. He compromised all the rest of his life, risked his signature without even knowing if he could honour it, and terrified by the anguish of the future, by the black misery which was going to descend on him, by the perspective of all the physical privations, and all the moral tortures, he went to get the new necklace, putting down on the shopkeeper's counter thirty-six thousand francs.

When Madame Loisel took back the necklace to Madame Forestier, the latter said to her with an offended expression:

"You ought to have given it back to me sooner, for I might have needed it."

And she did not open the case, as her friend had feared. If she had perceived the substitution, what would she have thought? What would she have said? Would she have taken her for a thief?

Madame Loisel experienced the horrible life of the poverty-stricken. She made her resolution, moreover, all at once, heroically. This frightful debt had to be paid. She would pay it. The maid was sent away; the flat was given up: an attic was rented up under the roofs.

She experienced the heavy work of a house, the hateful labours of a kitchen. She washed the dishes, wearing out her rosy nails on the greasy pottery and the bottoms of saucepans. She washed dirty linen, shirts, and towels, and hung them out to dry on a rope; she carried the rubbish down to the street every morning, and brought up the water, stopping at each flight to get her breath. And, dressed like a woman of the people, she went to the fruiterer's, the grocer's, the butcher's, with her basket on her arm, bargaining, insulted, defending penny by penny her wretched money.

Every month promissory notes had to be paid, others renewed, time asked for.

Her husband worked in the evening, setting in order a tradesman's accounts, and at night he often made copies at twenty-five centimes a page.

And this life lasted ten years.

At the end of ten years, they had paid back everything, everything, with the usury charges, and the accumulation of superimposed interest.

Madame Loisel seemed an old woman now. She had become the strong rough, hard woman of poor households. Her hair badly dressed, with her skirts uneven, and her hands red, she spoke in a loud voice, washed the floors in a swirl of water. But, sometimes, when her husband was at the office, she would sit beside the window, and she thought of the evening long ago, of that ball where she had been so beautiful and so admired. What would have happened if she had not lost that necklace? Who knows? Who knows? How queer life is, how easily changed! How small a thing it needs to destroy you, or to save you!

Now, one Sunday, when she had gone to take a turn in the Champs-Élysées as a relaxation after the toils of the week, she saw suddenly a lady taking a child out for a walk. It was Madame Forestier, still young, still beautiful, still seductive.

Madame Loisel felt moved. Was she going to speak to her? Why, yes. And now that she had paid she would tell her everything. Why not?

She went up to her.

"Good day, Jeanne."

The other did not recognize her, and was astonished at being addressed so familiarly by this woman. She stammered:

"But – Madame! I do not know— You must have made a mistake."

"No. I am Mathilde Loisel."

Her friend uttered a cry.

"Oh, my poor Mathilde! How you've changed!"

"Yes, I've gone through very hard days since I saw you: and much distress – and that because of you!"

"Me! How?"

"You remember that necklace of diamonds that you lent me to go to the ball at the Ministry."

"Yes. Well?"

"Well, I lost it."

"How? since you brought it back to me."

"I brought back another just the same. And for ten years we've been paying for it. You'll understand that it wasn't easy for us, we who have no money. At last it is done, and I am awfully glad."

Madame Forestier stood still.

"You say that you bought a diamond necklace to replace mine?"

"Yes. You didn't notice it, eh? They were very alike."

And she smiled a smile of proud, simple joy.

Madame Forestier, very affected, took her two hands.

"Oh, my poor Mathilde! But mine was imitation. It was worth at the most five hundred francs."

The Fiery Wooing of Mordred

P G Wodehouse

The pint of Lager breathed heavily through his nose.

"Silly fathead!" he said. "Ashtrays in every nook and cranny of the room – ashtrays staring you in the eye wherever you look – and he has to go and do a fool thing like that."

He was alluding to a young gentleman with a vacant, fish-like face who, leaving the bar-parlour of the Angler's Rest a few moments before, had thrown his cigarette into the wastepaper basket, causing it to burst into a cheerful blaze. Not one of the little company of amateur fire-fighters but was ruffled. A Small Bass with a high blood pressure had had to have his collar loosened, and the satin-clad bosom of Miss Postlethwaite, our emotional barmaid, was still heaving.

Only Mr Mulliner seemed disposed to take a tolerant view of what had occurred.

"In fairness to the lad," he pointed out, sipping his hot Scotch and lemon, "we must remember that our bar-parlour contains no grand piano or priceless old walnut table, which to the younger generation are the normal and natural reposi-tories for lighted cigarette-ends. Failing these, he, of course, selected the wastepaper basket. Like Mordred."

"Like who?" asked a Whisky and Splash.

"Whom," corrected Miss Postlethwaite.

The Whisky and Splash apologized.

"A nephew of mine. Mordred Mulliner, the poet."

"Mordred," murmured Miss Postlethwaite pensively. "A sweet name."

"And one," said Mr Mulliner, "that fitted him admirably, for he was a comely, lovable sensitive youth with large, fawn-like eyes, delicately chiselled features and excellent teeth. I mention these teeth, because it was owing to them that the train of events started which I am about to describe."

"He bit somebody?" queried Miss Postlethwaite, groping.

"No. But if he had had no teeth he would not have gone to the dentist's that day, and if he had not gone to the dentist's he would not have met Annabelle."

"Annabelle whom?"

"Who," corrected Miss Postlethwaite.

"Oh, shoot," said the Whisky and Splash.

"Annabelle Sprockett-Sprockett, the only daughter of Sir Murgatroyd and Lady Sprockett-Sprockett of Smattering Hall, Worcestershire. Impractical in many ways," said Mr Mulliner, "Mordred never failed to visit his dentist every six months, and on the morning on which my story opens he had just seated himself in the empty waiting-room and was turning the pages of a three-months-old copy of the *Tatler* when the door opened and there entered a girl at the sight of whom – or who, if our friend here prefers it – something seemed to explode on the left side of his chest like a bomb. The *Tatler* swam before his eyes, and when it solidified again he realized that love had come to him at last."

*   *   *

Most of the Mulliners (said Mr Mulliner) have fallen in love at first sight, but few with so good an excuse as Mordred. She was a singularly beautiful girl, and for a while it was this beauty of hers that enchained my nephew's attention to the exclusion of all else. It was only after he had sat gulping for some minutes like a dog with a chicken-bone in its throat that he detected the sadness in her face. He could see now that her eyes, as she listlessly perused her four-months-old copy of *Punch*, were heavy with pain.

His heart ached for her, and as there is something about the atmosphere of a dentist's waiting-room which breaks down the barriers of conventional etiquette he was emboldened to speak.

"Courage!" he said. "It may not be so bad, after all. He may just fool about with that little mirror thing of his, and decide that there is nothing that needs to be done."

For the first time she smiled – faintly, but with sufficient breath to give Mordred another powerful jolt.

"I'm not worrying about the dentist," she explained. "My trouble is that I live miles away in the country and only get a chance of coming to London about twice a year for about a couple of hours. I was hoping that I should be able to put in a long spell of window-shopping in Bond Street, but now I've got to wait goodness knows how long I don't suppose I shall have time to do a thing. My train goes at one-fifteen."

All the chivalry in Mordred came to the surface like a leaping trout.

"If you would care to take my place—"

"Oh, I couldn't."

"Please. I shall enjoy waiting. It will give me an opportunity of catching up with my reading."

"Well, if you really wouldn't mind—"

Considering that Mordred by this time was in the market to tackle dragons on her behalf or to climb the loftiest peak of the Alps to supply her with edelweiss, he was able to assure her that he did not mind. So in she went flashing at him a shy glance of gratitude which nearly doubled him up, and he lit a cigarette and fell into a reverie. And presently she came out and he sprang to his feet, courteously throwing his cigarette into the wastepaper basket.

She uttered a cry. Mordred recovered the cigarette.

"Silly of me," he said, with a deprecating laugh. "I'm always doing that. Absent-minded. I've burned two flats already this year."

She caught her breath.

"Burned to the ground?"

"Well, not to the ground. They were on the top floor."

"But you burned them?"

"Oh, yes. I burned them."

"Well, well!" She seemed to muse. "Well, goodbye, Mr—"

"Mulliner. Mordred Mulliner."

"Goodbye, Mr Mulliner, and thank you so much."

"Not at all, Miss—"

"Sprockett-Sprockett."

"Not at all, Miss Sprockett-Sprockett. A pleasure."

She passed from the room, and a few minutes later he was lying back in the dentist's chair, filled with an infinite sadness. This was not due to any activity on the part of the dentist, who had just said with a rueful sigh that there didn't seem to be anything to do this time, but to the fact that his life was now a blank. He loved this beautiful girl, and he would never see her more. It was just another case of ships that pass in the waiting-room. Conceive his astonishment, therefore, when by the afternoon post next day he received a letter which ran as follows:

> Smattering Hall,
>> Lower Smattering-on-the-Wissel,
>>> Worcestershire.

DEAR MR MULLINER,

My little girl has told me how very kind you were to her at the dentist's today. I cannot tell you how grateful she was. She does so love to walk down Bond Street and breathe on the jewellers' windows, and but for you she would have had to go another six months without her little treat.

I suppose you are a very busy man, like everybody in London, but if you can spare the time it would give my husband and myself so much pleasure if you could run down and stay with us for a few days – a long weekend, or even longer if you can manage it.

With best wishes,
> Yours sincerely,
>> AURELIA SPROCKETT-SPROCKETT.

Mordred read this communication six times in a minute and a quarter and then seventeen times rather more slowly in order to savour any *nuance* of it that he might have over-looked. He took it that the girl must have got his address from the dentist's secretary on her way out, and he was doubly thrilled – first, by this evidence that one so lovely was as intelligent as she was beautiful, and secondly because the whole thing seemed to him so frightfully significant. A girl, he meant to say, does not get her mother to invite fellows to her country home for long weekends (or even longer if they can manage it) unless such fellows have made a pretty substantial hit with her. This, he contended, stood to reason.

He hastened to the nearest post-office, despatched a telegram to Lady Sprockett-Sprockett assuring her that he would be with her on the morrow, and returned to his flat to pack his effects. His heart was singing within him. Apart from anything else, the invitation could not have come at a more fortunate moment, for what with musing of his great love while smoking cigarettes he had practically gutted his little nest of the previous evening, and while it was still hab-itable in a sense there was no gainsaying the fact that all those charred sofas and things struck a rather melancholy note and he would be glad to be away from it all for a few days.

It seemed to Mordred, as he travelled down on the follow-ing afternoon, that the wheels of the train, clattering over the metals, were singing "Sprockett-Sprockett" – not "Annabelle", of course, for he did not yet know her name – and it was with a whispered "Sprockett-Sprockett" on his lips

35

that he alighted at the little station of Smattering-cum-Blimpstead-in-the-Vale, which, as his hostess's notepaper had informed him, was where you got off for the Hall. And when he perceived that the girl herself had come to meet him in a two-seater car the whisper nearly became a shout.

For perhaps three minutes, as he sat beside her, Mordred remained in this condition of ecstatic bliss. Here he was, he reflected, and here she was — here, in fact, they both were — together, and he was just about to point out how jolly this was and — if he could work it without seeming to rush things too much — to drop a hint to the effect that he could wish this state of affairs to continue through all eternity, when the girl drew up outside a tobacconist's.

"I won't be a minute," she said. "I promised Biffy I would bring him back some cigarettes."

A cold hand seemed to lay itself on Mordred's heart.

"Biffy?"

"Captain Biffing, one of the men at the Hall. And Guffy wants some pipe-cleaners."

"Guffy?"

"Jack Guffington. I expect you know his name, if you are interested in racing. He was third in last year's Grand National."

"Is he staying at the Hall, too?"

"Yes."

"You have a large house-party?"

"Oh, not so very. Let me see. There's Billy Biffing, Jack Guffington, Ted Prosser, Freddie Boot — he's the tennis champion of the county, Tommy Mainprice, and – oh, yes, Algy Fripp – the big-game hunter, you know."

The hand on Mordred's heart, now definitely iced, tightened its grip. With a lover's sanguine optimism, he had supposed that this visit of his was going to be just three days of jolly sylvan solitude with Annabelle Sprockett-Sprockett. And now it appeared that the place was unwholesomely crowded with his fellow men. And what fellow men! Big-game hunters... Tennis champions... Chaps who rode in Grand Nationals... He could see them in his mind's eye – lean, wiry, riding-breeched and flannel-trousered young Apollos, any one of them capable of cutting out his weight in Clark Gables.

A faint hope stirred within him.

"You have also, of course, with you Mrs Biffing, Mrs Guffington, Mrs Prosser, Mrs Boot, Mrs Mainprice and Mrs Algernon Fripp?"

"Oh, no, they aren't married."

"None of them?"

"No."

The faint hope coughed quietly and died.

"Ah," said Mordred.

While the girl was in the shop, he remained brooding. The fact that not one of these blisters should be married filled him with an austere disapproval. If they had had the least spark of civic sense, he felt, they would have taken on the duties and responsibilities of matrimony years ago. But no. Intent upon their selfish pleasures, they had callously remained bachelors. It was this spirit of *laissez-faire*, Mordred considered, that was eating like a canker into the soul of England.

He was aware of Annabelle standing beside him.

"Eh?" he said, starting.

"I was saying: 'Have you plenty of cigarettes?'"

"Plenty, thank you."

"Good. And of course there will be a box in your room. Men always like to smoke in their bedrooms, don't they? As a matter of fact, two boxes – Turkish and Virginian. Father put them there specially."

"Very kind of him," said Mordred mechanically.

He relapsed into a moody silence, and they drove off.

It would be agreeable (said Mr Mulliner) if, having shown you my nephew so gloomy, so apprehensive, so tortured with dark forebodings at this juncture, I were able now to state that the hearty English welcome of Sir Murgatroyd and Lady Sprockett-Sprockett on his arrival at the Hall cheered him up and put new life into him. Nothing, too, would give me greater pleasure than to say that he found, on encountering the dreaded Biffies and Guffies, that they were negligible little runts with faces incapable of inspiring affection in any good woman.

But I must adhere rigidly to the facts. Genial, even effusive, though his host and hostess showed themselves, their cordiality left him cold. And, so far from his rivals being weeds, they were one and all models of manly beauty, and the spectacle of their obvious worship of Annabelle cut my nephew like a knife.

And on top of all this there was Smattering Hall itself.

Smattering Hall destroyed Mordred's last hope. It was one of those vast edifices, so common throughout the countryside of England, whose original founders seem to have budgeted for families of twenty-five or so and a domestic staff of not less than a hundred. "Home isn't home," one can picture them saying to themselves, "unless you have plenty of elbow room." And so this huge, majestic pile had come into being. Romantic persons, confronted with it, thought of knights in armour riding forth to the Crusades. More earthly individuals felt that it must cost a packet to keep up. Mordred's reaction on passing through the front door was a sort of sick sensation, a kind of settled despair.

How, he asked himself, even assuming that by some miracle he succeeded in fighting his way to her heart through all these Biffies and Guffies, could he ever dare to take Annabelle from a home like this? He had quite satisfactory private means, of course, and would be able, when married, to give up the bachelor flat and spread himself to something on a bigger scale – possibly, if sufficiently *bijou*, even a desirable residence in the Mayfair district. But after Smattering Hall would not Annabelle feel like a sardine in the largest of London houses?

Such were the dark thoughts that raced through Mordred's brain before, during and after dinner. At eleven o'clock he pleaded fatigue after his journey, and Sir Murgatroyd accompanied him to his room, anxious, like a good host, to see that everything was comfortable.

"Very sensible of you to turn in early," he said, in his bluff, genial way. "So many young men ruin their health with late hours. Now you, I imagine, will just get into a dressing-gown and smoke a cigarette or two and have the light out by twelve. You have plenty of cigarettes? I told them to see that you were well supplied. I always think the bedroom smoke is the best one of the day. Nobody to disturb you, and all that. If you want to write letters or anything, there is lots of paper, and here is the wastepaper basket, which is always so necessary. Well, good night, my boy, good night."

The door closed, and Mordred, as foreshadowed, got into a dressing-gown and lit a cigarette. But though, having done this, he made his way to the writing-table, it was not with any idea of getting abreast of his correspondence. It was his purpose to compose a poem to Annabelle Sprockett-Sprockett. He had felt it seething within him all the evening, and sleep would be impossible until it was out of his system.

Hitherto, I should mention, my nephew's poetry, for he belonged to the modern fearless school, had always been stark and rhymeless and had dealt principally with corpses and the smell of cooking cabbage. But now, with the moonlight silvering the balcony outside, he found that his mind had become full of words like "love" and "dove" and "eyes" and "summer skies".

Blue eyes, wrote Mordred...
   Sweet lips, wrote Mordred...
Oh, eyes like skies of summer blue...
Oh, love...
Oh, dove...
Oh, lips...

With a muttered ejaculation of chagrin he tore the sheet across and threw it into the wastepaper basket.

Blue eyes that burn into my soul,
    Sweet lips that smile my heart away
Pom-pom, pom-pom, pom something whole (Goal?)
    And tiddly-iddly-umpty-ay. (Gay? Say? Happy day?)

Blue eyes into my soul that burn,
    Sweet lips that smile away my heart,
Oh, something something turn or yearn
    And something something something part.

You burn into my soul, blue eyes,
You smile my heart away, sweet lips,
Short long short long of summer skies
    And something something something trips.
    (Hips? Ships? Pips?)

He threw the sheet into the wastepaper basket and rose with a stifled oath. The wastepaper basket was nearly full now, and still his poet's sense told him that he had not achieved perfection. He thought he saw the reason for this. You can't just sit in a chair and expect inspiration to flow — you want to walk about and clutch your hair and snap your fingers. It had been his intention to pace the room, but the moonlight pouring in through the open window called to him. He went out on to the balcony. It was but a short distance to the dim, mysterious lawn. Impulsively he dropped from the stone balustrade.

The effect was magical. Stimulated by the improved conditions, his Muse gave quick service, and this time he saw at once that she had rung the bell and delivered the goods. One turn up and down the lawn, and he was reciting as follows:

TO ANNABELLE

Oh, lips that smile! Oh, eyes that shine
Like summer skies, or stars above!
Your beauty maddens me like wine,
Oh, umpty-pumpty-tumty love!

And he was just wondering, for he was a severe critic of his own work, whether that last line couldn't be polished up a bit, when his eye was attracted by something that shone like summer skies or stars above and, looking more closely, he perceived that his bedroom curtains were on fire.

Now, I will not pretend that my nephew Mordred was in every respect the cool-headed man of action, but this happened to be a situation with which use had familiarized him. He knew the procedure.

"Fire!" he shouted.

A head appeared in an upstairs window. He recognized it as that of Captain Biffing.

"Eh?" said Captain Biffing.

"Fire!"

"What?"

"Fire!" vociferated Mordred. "F for Francis, I for Isabel…"

"Oh, fire?" said Captain Biffing. "Right ho."

And presently the house began to discharge its occupants.

In the proceedings which followed, Mordred, I fear, did not appear to the greatest advantage. This is an age of specialization, and if you take the specialist off his own particular ground he is at a loss. Mordred's genius, as we have seen, lay in the direction of starting fires. Putting them out called for quite different qualities, and these he did not possess. On the various occasions of holocausts at his series of flats, he had never attempted to play an active part, contenting himself with going downstairs and asking the janitor to step up and see what he could do about it. So now, though under the bright eyes of Annabelle Sprockett-Sprockett he would have given much to be able to dominate the scene, the truth is that the Biffies and Guffies simply played him off the stage.

His heart sank as he noted the hideous efficiency of these young men. They called for buckets. They formed a line. Freddie Boot leaped lissomely on to the balcony, and Algy Fripp, mounted on a wheelbarrow, handed up to him the necessary supplies. And after Mordred, trying to do his bit, had tripped up Jack Guffington and upset two buckets over Ted Prosser he was advised in set terms to withdraw into the background and stay there.

It was a black ten minutes for the unfortunate young man. One glance at Sir Murgatroyd's twisted face as he watched the operations was enough to tell him how desperately anxious the fine old man was for the safety of his ancestral home and how bitter would be his resentment against the person who had endangered it. And the same applied to Lady

Sprockett-Sprockett and Annabelle. Mordred could see the anxiety in their eyes, and the thought that ere long those eyes must be turned accusingly on him chilled him to the marrow.

Presently, Freddie Boot emerged from the bedroom to announce that all was well.

"It's out," he said, jumping lightly down. "Anybody know whose room it was?"

Mordred felt a sickening qualm, but the splendid Mulliner courage sustained him. He stepped forward, white and tense.

"Mine," he said.

He became the instant centre of attention. The six young men looked at him.

"Yours?"

"Oh, yours, was it?"

"What happened?"

"How did it start?"

"Yes, how did it start?"

"Must have started somehow, I mean," said Captain Biffing, who was a clear thinker. "I mean to say, must have, don't you know, what?"

Mordred mastered his voice.

"I was smoking, and I suppose I threw my cigarette into the wastepaper basket, and as it was full of paper..."

"Full of paper? Why was it full of paper?"

"I had been writing a poem."

There was a stir of bewilderment.

"A what?" said Ted Prosser.

"Writing a what?" said Jack Guffington.

"Writing a *poem?*" asked Captain Biffing of Tommy Main-price.

"That's how I got the story," said Tommy Mainprice, plainly shaken.

"Chap was writing a poem," Freddie Boot informed Algy Fripp.

"You mean the chap writes poems?"

"That's right. Poems."

"Well, I'm dashed!"

"Well, I'm blowed!"

Their now unconcealed scorn was hard to bear. Mordred chafed beneath it. The word "poem" was flitting from lip to lip, and it was only too evident that, had there been an "s" in the word, those present would have hissed it. Reason told him that these men were mere clods, Philistines, fatheads who would not recognize the rare and the beautiful if you handed it to them on a skewer, but that did not seem to make it any better. He knew that he should be scorning them, but it is not easy to go about scorning people in a dressing-gown, especially if you have no socks on and the night breeze is cool around the ankles. So, as I say, he chafed. And finally, when he saw the butler bend down with pursed lips to the ear of the cook, who was a little hard of hearing, and after a contemptuous glance in his direction speak into it, spacing his syllables carefully, something within him seemed to snap.

"I regret, Sir Murgatroyd," he said, "that urgent family business compels me to return to London immediately. I shall be obliged to take the first train in the morning."

Without another word he went into the house.

In the matter of camping out in devastated areas my nephew had, of course, become by this time an old hand. It was rarely nowadays that a few ashes and cinders about the place disturbed him. But when he had returned to his bedroom one look was enough to assure him that nothing practical in the way of sleep was to be achieved here. Apart from the unpleasant, acrid smell of burned poetry, the apartment, thanks to the efforts of Freddie Boot, had been converted into a kind of inland sea. The carpet was awash, and on the bed only a duck could have made itself at home.

And so it came about that some ten minutes later Mordred Mulliner lay stretched upon a high-backed couch in the library, endeavouring by means of counting sheep jumping through a gap in a hedge to lull himself into unconsciousness.

But sleep refused to come. Nor in his heart had he really thought that it would. When the human soul is on the rack, it cannot just curl up and close its eyes and expect to get its eight hours as if nothing had happened. It was all very well for Mordred to count sheep, but what did this profit him when each sheep in turn assumed the features and lineaments of Annabelle Sprockett-Sprockett and, what was more, gave him a reproachful glance as it drew itself together for the spring?

Remorse gnawed him. He was tortured by a wild regret for what might have been. He was not saying that with all these Biffies and Guffies in the field he had ever had more than a hundred to eight chance of winning that lovely girl, but at least his hat had been in the ring. Now it was definitely out. Dreamy Mordred may have been – romantic – impractical – but he had enough sense to see that the very worst thing you can do when you are trying to make a favourable impression on the adored object is to set fire to her childhood home, every stick and stone of which she has no doubt worshipped since they put her into rompers.

He had reached this point in his meditations, and was about to send his two hundred and thirty-second sheep at the gap, when with a suddenness which affected him much as an explosion of gelignite would have done, the lights flashed on. For an instant, he lay quivering, then, cautiously poking his head round the corner of the couch, he looked to see who his visitors were.

It was a little party of three that had entered the room. First came Sir Murgatroyd, carrying a tray of sandwiches. He was followed by Lady Sprockett-Sprockett with a syphon and glasses. The rear was brought up by Annabelle, who was bearing a bottle of whisky and two dry ginger ales.

So evident was it that they were assembling here for purposes of a family council that, but for one circumstance, Mordred, to whom anything in the nature of eavesdropping was as repugnant as it has always been to all the Mulliners, would have sprung up with a polite "Excuse me" and taken his blanket elsewhere. This circumstance was the fact that on lying down he had kicked his slippers under the couch, well out of reach. The soul of modesty, he could not affront Annabelle with the spectacle of his bare toes.

So he lay there in silence, and silence, broken only by the

swishing of soda-water and the *whoosh* of opened ginger-ale bottles, reigned in the room beyond.

Then Sir Murgatroyd spoke.

"Well, that's that," he said, bleakly.

There was a gurgle as Lady Sprockett-Sprockett drank ginger ale. Then her quiet, well-bred voice broke the pause.

"Yes," she said, "it is the end."

"The end," agreed Sir Murgatroyd heavily. "No good trying to struggle on against luck like ours. Here we are and here we have got to stay, mouldering on in this blasted barrack of a place which eats up every penny of my income when, but for the fussy interference of that gang of officious, ugly nitwits, there would have been nothing left of it but a pile of ashes, with a man from the Insurance Company standing on it with his fountain-pen, writing cheques. Curse those imbeciles! Did you see that young Fripp with those buckets?"

"I did, indeed," sighed Lady Sprockett-Sprockett.

"Annabelle," said Sir Murgatroyd sharply.

"Yes, Father?"

"It has seemed to me lately, watching you with a father's eye, that you have shown signs of being attracted by young Algernon Fripp. Let me tell you that if ever you allow yourself to be ensnared by his insidious wiles, or by those of William Biffing, John Guffington, Edward Prosser, Thomas Mainprice or Frederick Boot, you will do so over my dead body. After what occurred tonight, those young men shall never darken my door again. They and their buckets! To think that we could have gone and lived in London..."

"In a nice little flat..." said Lady Sprockett-Sprockett.

"Handy for my club…"

"Convenient for the shops…"

"Within a stone's throw of the theatres…"

"Seeing all our friends…"

"Had it not been," said Sir Murgatroyd, summing up, "for the pestilential activities of these Guffingtons, these Biffings, these insufferable Fripps, men who ought never to be trusted near a bucket of water when a mortgaged country-house has got nicely alight. I did think," proceeded the stricken old man, helping himself to a sandwich, "that when Annabelle, with a ready intelligence which I cannot overpraise, realized this young Mulliner's splendid gifts and made us ask him down here, the happy ending was in sight. What Smattering Hall has needed for generations has been a man who throws his cigarette-ends into wastepaper baskets. I was convinced that here at last was the angel of mercy we required."

"He did his best, Father."

"No man could have done more," agreed Sir Murgatroyd cordially. "The way he upset those buckets and kept getting entangled in people's legs. Very shrewd. It thrilled me to see him. I don't know when I've met a young fellow I liked and respected more. And what if he is a poet? Poets are all right. Why, dash it, I'm a poet myself. At the last dinner of the Loyal Sons of Worcestershire I composed a poem which, let me tell you, was pretty generally admired. I read it out to the boys over the port, and they cheered me to the echo. It was about a young lady of Bewdley, who sometimes behaved rather rudely…"

"Not before Mother, Father."

"Perhaps you're right. Well, I'm off to bed. Come along, Aurelia. You coming, Annabelle?"

"Not yet, Father. I want to stay and think."

"Do what?"

"Think."

"Oh, think? Well, all right."

"But, Murgatroyd," said Lady Sprockett-Sprockett, "is there no hope? After all, there are plenty of cigarettes in the house, and we could always give Mr Mulliner another waste-paper basket..."

"No good. You heard him say he was leaving by the first train tomorrow. When I think that we shall never see that splendid young man again... Why, hullo, hullo, hullo, what's this? Crying, Annabelle?"

"Oh, Mother!"

"My darling, what is it?"

A choking sob escaped the girl.

"Mother, I love him! Directly I saw him in the dentist's waiting-room, something seemed to go all over me, and I knew that there could be no other man for me. And, now..."

"Hi!" cried Mordred, popping up over the side of the couch like a jack-in-the-box.

He had listened with growing understanding to the conversation which I have related, but had shrunk from revealing his presence because, as I say, his toes were bare. But this was too much. Toes or no toes, he felt that he must be in this.

"You love me, Annabelle?" he cried.

His sudden advent had occasioned, I need scarcely say, a

certain reaction in those present. Sir Murgatroyd had leaped like a jumping bean. Lady Sprockett-Sprockett had quivered like a jelly. As for Annabelle, her lovely mouth was open to the extent of perhaps three inches, and she was staring like one who sees a vision.

"You really love me, Annabelle?"

"Yes, Mordred."

"Sir Murgatroyd," said Mordred formally, "I have the honour to ask you for your daughter's hand. I am only a poor poet…"

"How poor?" asked the other, keenly.

"I was referring to my Art," explained Mordred. "Financially, I am nicely fixed. I could support Annabelle in modest comfort."

"Then take her, my boy, take her. You will live, of course" – the old man winced – "in London?"

"Yes. And so shall you."

Sir Murgatroyd shook his head.

"No, no, that dream is ended. It is true that in certain circumstances I had hoped to do so, for the insurance, I may mention, amounts to as much as a hundred thousand pounds, but I am resigned now to spending the rest of my life in this infernal family vault. I see no reprieve."

"I understand," said Mordred, nodding. "You mean you have no paraffin in the house?"

Sir Murgatroyd started.

"Paraffin?"

"If," said Mordred, and his voice was very gentle and winning, "there had been paraffin on the premises, I think it

51

possible that tonight's conflagration, doubtless imperfectly quenched, might have broken out again, this time with more serious results. It is often this way with fires. You pour buckets of water on them and think they are extinguished, but all the time they have been smouldering unnoticed, to break out once more in – well, in here for example."

"Or the billiard-room," said Lady Sprockett-Sprockett.

"*And* the billiard-room," corrected Sir Murgatroyd.

"And the billiard-room," said Mordred. "And possibly – who knows? – in the drawing-room, dining-room, kitchen, servants' hall, butler's pantry and the usual domestic offices, as well. Still, as you say you have no paraffin…"

"My boy," said Sir Murgatroyd, in a shaking voice, "what gave you the idea that we have no paraffin? How did you fall into this odd error? We have gallons of paraffin. The cellar is full of it."

"And Annabelle will show you the way to the cellar – in case you thought of going there," said Lady Sprockett-Sprockett. "Won't you, dear?"

"Of course, Mother. You will like the cellar, Mordred, darling. Most picturesque. Possibly, if you are interested in paraffin, you might also care to take a look at our little store of paper and shavings, too."

"My angel," said Mordred, tenderly, "you think of everything."

He found his slippers, and hand in hand they passed down the stairs. Above them, they could see the head of Sir Murgatroyd, as he leaned over the banisters. A box of matches fell at their feet like a father's benediction.

How Un-American Can You Get?

Art Buchwald

I have a confession to make, and the sooner it gets out in the open, the better I'll feel about it. *I don't drive a car.*

Americans are broad-minded people. They'll accept the fact that a person can be an alcoholic, a dope fiend, a wife beater, and even a newspaperman, but if a man doesn't drive, there is something wrong with him.

Through the years I've found it very embarrassing to admit it to anyone, and my best friends tend to view me with suspicion and contempt.

But where I really run into trouble is when I go into a store and try to make a purchase with a check.

It happened again last week when I went to a discount house at a large shopping center in Maryland. I wanted to buy a portable typewriter, and the salesman was very helpful about showing me the different models.

I decided on one, and then I said, "May I write out a personal check?"

"Naturally," he said kindly. "Do you have any identification?"

"Of course," I said. I produced an American Express credit card, a Diners' Club credit card, a Carte Blanche credit card, a Bell Telephone credit card, and my pass to the White House.

The man inspected them all and then said, "Where's your driver's license?"

"I don't have one," I replied.

"Did you lose it?"

"No, I didn't lose it. I don't drive a car."

He pushed a button under the cash register, and suddenly a floor manager came rushing over.

The salesman had now become surly. "This guy's trying to cash a check, and he doesn't have a driver's license. Should I call the store detective?"

"Wait a minute. I'll talk to him," the manager said. "Did you lose your driver's license for some traffic offense?"

"No, I've never driven. I don't like to drive."

"Nobody likes to drive," the floor manager shouted. "That's no excuse. Why are you trying to cash a check if you don't have a driver's license?"

"I thought all the other identification was good enough. I had to be cleared by the Secret Service to get this White House pass," I said hopefully.

The floor manager looked scornfully at the pass and all my credit cards. "Anyone can get cleared by the Secret Service. Hey, wait a minute. How did you get out here to the shopping center if you don't drive?"

"I took a taxi," I said.

"Well, that takes the cake," he said.

By this time a crowd had gathered.

"What happened?"

"Guy doesn't have a driver's license."

"Says he doesn't even drive. Never has driven."

"Lynch him."

"Tar and feather him."

"How un-American can you get?"

The crowd was getting ugly, so I decided to forget the typewriter.

"Never mind," I said. "I'll go somewhere else."

By this time the president of the store had arrived on the scene. Fortunately, he recognized my name and okayed the check. He was very embarrassed by the treatment I had received and said, "Come on, I'll buy you a drink."

"I forgot to tell you," I said. "I don't drink either."

This was too much, even for him, and he pushed me toward the door.

"Get out of here," he said, "and don't come back!"

The Rocking-Horse Winner

D H Lawrence

There was a woman who was beautiful, who started with all the advantages, yet she had no luck. She married for love, and the love turned to dust. She had bonny children, yet she felt they had been thrust upon her, and she could not love them. They looked at her coldly, as if they were finding fault with her. And hurriedly she felt she must cover up some fault in herself. Yet what it was that she must cover up she never knew. Nevertheless, when her children were present, she always felt the centre of her heart go hard. This troubled her, and in her manner she was all the more gentle and anxious for her children, as if she loved them very much. Only she herself knew that at the centre of her heart was a hard little place that could not feel love, no, not for anybody. Everybody else said of her: "She is such a good mother. She adores her children." Only she herself, and her children themselves, knew it was not so. They read it in each other's eyes.

There were a boy and two little girls. They lived in a pleasant house, with a garden, and they had discreet servants, and felt themselves superior to anyone in the neighbourhood.

Although they lived in style, they felt always an anxiety in the house. There was never enough money. The mother had a small income, and the father had a small income, but not nearly enough, for the social position which they had to keep up. The father went into town to some office. But though he had good prospects, these prospects never materialized. There was always the grinding sense of the shortage of money, though the style was always kept up.

At last the mother said, "I will see if *I* can't make something." But she did not know where to begin. She racked her brains, and tried this thing and the other, but could not find anything successful. The failure made deep lines come into her face. Her children were growing up, they would have to go to school. There must be more money, there must be more money. The father, who was always very handsome and expensive in his tastes, seemed as if he never *would* be able to do anything worth doing. And the mother, who had a great belief in herself, did not succeed any better, and her tastes were just as expensive.

And so the house came to be haunted by the unspoken phrase: *There must be more money! There must be more money!* The children could hear it all the time, though nobody said it aloud. They heard it at Christmas, when the expensive and splendid toys filled the nursery. Behind the shining modern rocking-horse, behind the smart doll's house, a voice would start whispering: "There *must* be more money! There *must* be more money!" And the children would stop playing, to listen for a moment. They would look into each other's eyes, to see if they had all heard. And each one saw in the eyes of the other two that they too had heard. "There *must* be more money! There *must* be more money!"

It came whispering from the springs of the still-swaying rocking-horse, and even the horse, bending his wooden, champing head, heard it. The big doll, sitting so pink and smirking in her new pram, could hear it quite plainly, and seemed to be smirking all the more self-consciously because of it. The foolish puppy, too, that took the place of the teddy-bear, he was looking so extraordinarily foolish for no other reason but that he heard the secret whisper all over the house: "There *must* be more money!"

Yet nobody ever said it aloud. The whisper was everywhere, and therefore no one spoke it. Just as no one ever says: "We are breathing!" in spite of the fact that breath is coming and going all the time.

"Mother," said the boy Paul one day, "why don't we keep a car of our own? Why do we always use uncle's, or else a taxi?"

"Because we're the poor members of the family," said the mother.

"But why *are* we, mother?"

"Well — I suppose," she said slowly and bitterly, "it's because your father has no luck."

The boy was silent for some time.

"Is luck money, mother?" he asked, rather timidly.

"No, Paul! Not quite. It's what causes you to have money."

"Oh!" said Paul vaguely. "I thought when Uncle Oscar said *filthy lucker*, it meant money."

"*Filthy lucre* does mean money," said the mother. "But it's lucre, not luck."

"Oh!" said the boy. "Then what *is* luck, mother?"

"It's what causes you to have money. If you're lucky you have money. That's why it's better to be born lucky than rich. If you're rich, you may lose your money. But if you're lucky, you will always get more money."

"Oh! Will you? And is father not lucky?"

"Very unlucky, I should say," she said bitterly.

The boy watched her with unsure eyes.

"Why?" he asked.

"I don't know. Nobody ever knows why one person is lucky and another unlucky."

"Don't they? Nobody at all? Does *nobody* know?"

"Perhaps God! But He never tells."

"He ought to, then. And aren't you lucky either, mother?"

"I can't be, if I married an unlucky husband."

"But by yourself, aren't you?"

"I used to think I was, before I married. Now I think I am very unlucky indeed."

"Why?"

"Well — never mind! Perhaps I'm not really," she said.

The child looked at her to see if she meant it. But he saw, by the lines of her mouth, that she was only trying to hide something from him.

"Well, anyhow," he said stoutly, "I'm a lucky person."

"Why?" said his mother, with a sudden laugh.

He stared at her. He didn't even know why he had said it.

"God told me," he asserted, brazening it out.

"I hope He did, dear!" she said, again with a laugh, but rather bitter.

"He did, mother!"

"Excellent!" said the mother, using one of her husband's exclamations.

The boy saw she did not believe him; or rather, that she paid no attention to this assertion. This angered him somewhere, and made him want to compel her attention.

He went off by himself, vaguely, in a childish way, seeking for the clue to "luck". Absorbed, taking no heed of other people, he went about with a sort of stealth, seeking inwardly for luck. He wanted luck, he wanted it, he wanted it. When the two girls were playing dolls in the nursery, he would sit on his big rocking-horse, charging madly into space, with a frenzy that made the little girls peer at him uneasily. Wildly the horse careered, the waving dark hair of the boy tossed, his eyes had a strange glare in them. The little girls dared not speak to him.

When he had ridden to the end of his mad little journey, he climbed down and stood in front of his rocking-horse; staring fixedly into its lowered face. Its red mouth was slightly open, its big eye was wide and glassy bright.

"Now!" he would silently command the snorting steed. "Now take me to where there is luck! Now take me!"

And he would slash the horse on the neck with the little whip he had asked Uncle Oscar for. He *knew* the horse could take him to where there was luck, if only he forced it. So he would mount again and start on his furious ride, hoping at last to get there. He knew he could get there.

"You'll break your horse, Paul!" said the nurse.

"He's always riding like that! I wish he'd leave off!" said his elder sister Joan.

But he only glared down on them in silence. Nurse gave him up. She could make nothing of him. Anyhow, he was growing beyond her.

One day his mother and his Uncle Oscar came in when he was on one of his furious rides. He did not speak to them.

"Hallo, you young jockey! Riding a winner?" said his uncle.

"Aren't you growing too big for a rocking-horse? You're not a very little boy any longer, you know," said his mother.

But Paul only gave a blue glare from his big, rather close-set eyes. He would speak to nobody when he was in full tilt. His mother watched him with an anxious expression on her face.

At last he suddenly stopped forcing his horse into the mechanical gallop, and slid down.

"Well, I got there!" he announced fiercely, his blue eyes still flaring, and his sturdy long legs straddling apart.

"Where did you get to?" asked his mother.

"Where I wanted to go," he flared back at her.

"That's right, son!" said Uncle Oscar. "Don't you stop till you get there. What's the horse's name?"

"He doesn't have a name," said the boy.

"Gets on without all right?" asked the uncle.

"Well, he has different names. He was called Sansovino last week."

"Sansovino, eh? Won at Ascot. How did you know this name?"

"He always talks about horse-races with Bassett," said Joan.

The uncle was delighted to find that his small nephew was posted with all the racing news. Bassett, the young gardener who had been wounded in the left foot in the war, and had got his present job through Oscar Cresswell, whose batman he had been, was a perfect blade of the "turf". He lived in the racing events, and the small boy lived with him.

Oscar Cresswell got it all from Bassett.

"Master Paul comes and asks me, so I can't do more than tell him, sir," said Bassett, his face terribly serious, as if he were speaking of religious matters.

"And does he ever put anything on a horse he fancies?"

"Well – I don't want to give him away – he's a young sport, a fine sport, sir. Would you mind asking him yourself? He sort of takes a pleasure in it, and perhaps he'd feel I was giving him away, sir, if you don't mind."

Bassett was serious as a church.

The uncle went back to his nephew and took him off for a ride in the car.

"Say, Paul, old man, do you ever put anything on a horse?" the uncle asked.

The boy watched the handsome man closely.

"Why, do you think I oughtn't to?" he parried.

"Not a bit of it! I thought perhaps you might give me a tip for the Lincoln."

The car sped on into the country, going down to Uncle Oscar's place in Hampshire.

"Honour bright?" said the nephew.

"Honour bright, son!" said the uncle.

"Well, then, Daffodil."

"Daffodil! I doubt it, sonny. What about Mirza?"

"I only know the winner," said the boy. "That's Daffodil."

"Daffodil, eh?"

There was a pause. Daffodil was an obscure horse comparatively.

"Uncle!"

"Yes, son?"

"You won't let it go any further, will you? I promised Bassett."

"Bassett be damned, old man! What's he got to do with it?"

"We're partners! We've been partners from the first! Uncle, he lent me my first five shillings, which I lost. I promised him, honour bright, it was only between me and him; only you gave me that ten-shilling note I started winning with, so I thought you were lucky. You won't let it go any further, will you?"

The boy gazed at his uncle from those big, hot, blue eyes, set rather close together. The uncle stirred and laughed uneasily.

"Right you are, son! I'll keep your tip private. Daffodil, eh? How much are you putting on him?"

"All except twenty pounds," said the boy. "I keep that in reserve."

The uncle thought it a good joke.

"You keep twenty pounds in reserve, do you, you young romancer? What are you betting, then?"

"I'm betting three hundred," said the boy gravely. "But it's between you and me, Uncle Oscar! Honour bright?"

The uncle burst into a roar of laughter.

"It's between you and me all right, you young Nat Gould," he said, laughing. "But where's your three hundred?"

"Bassett keeps it for me. We're partners."

"You are, are you! And what is Bassett putting on Daffodil?"

"He won't go quite as high as I do, I expect. Perhaps he'll go a hundred and fifty."

"What, pennies?" laughed the uncle.

"Pounds," said the child, with a surprised look at his uncle. "Bassett keeps a bigger reserve than I do."

Between wonder and amusement, Uncle Oscar was silent. He pursued the matter no further, but he determined to take his nephew with him to the Lincoln races.

"Now, son," he said, "I'm putting twenty on Mirza, and I'll put five on for you on any horse you fancy. What's your pick?"

"Daffodil, uncle!"

"No, not the fiver on Daffodil!"

"I should if it was my own fiver," said the child.

"Good! Good! Right you are! A fiver for me and a fiver for you on Daffodil."

The child had never been to a race-meeting before, and his eyes were blue fire. He pursed his mouth tight and watched. A Frenchman just in front had put his money on Lancelot. Wild with excitement, he flayed his arms up and down, yelling *Lancelot! Lancelot!* in his French accent.

Daffodil came in first, Lancelot second, Mirza third. The

child, flushed and with eyes blazing, was curiously serene. His uncle brought him four five-pound notes: four to one.

"What am I to do with these?" he cried, waving them before the boy's eyes.

"I suppose we'll talk to Bassett," said the boy. "I expect I have fifteen hundred now, and twenty in reserve; and this twenty."

His uncle studied him for some moments.

"Look here, son!" he said. "You're not serious about Bassett and that fifteen hundred, are you?"

"Yes, I am. But it's between you and me, uncle. Honour bright?"

"Honour bright all right, son! But I must talk to Bassett."

"If you'd like to be a partner, uncle, with Bassett and me, we could all be partners. Only, you'd have to promise, honour bright, uncle, not to let it go beyond us three. Bassett and I are lucky, and you must be lucky, because it was your ten shillings I started winning with..."

Uncle Oscar took both Bassett and Paul into Richmond Park for an afternoon, and there they talked.

"It's like this, you see, sir," Bassett said. "Master Paul would get me talking about racing events, spinning yarns, you know, sir. And he was always keen on knowing if I'd made or if I'd lost. It's about a year since, now, that I put five shillings on Blush of Dawn for him: and we lost. Then the luck turned, with that ten shillings he had from you: that we put on Singhalese. And since that time, it's been pretty steady, all things considering. What do you say, Master Paul?"

"We're all right when we're *sure*," said Paul. "It's when we're not quite sure that we go down."

"Oh, but we're careful then," said Bassett.

"But when are you *sure?*" smiled Uncle Oscar.

"It's Master Paul, sir," said Bassett in a secret, religious voice. "It's as if he had it from heaven. Like Daffodil, now, for the Lincoln. That was as sure as eggs."

"Did you put anything on Daffodil?" asked Oscar Cresswell.

"Yes, sir. I made my bit."

"And my nephew?"

Bassett was obstinately silent, looking at Paul.

"I made twelve hundred, didn't I, Bassett? I told uncle I was putting three hundred on Daffodil."

"That's right," said Bassett, nodding.

"But where's the money?" asked the uncle.

"I keep it safe locked up, sir. Master Paul, he can have it any minute he likes to ask for it."

"What, fifteen hundred pounds?"

"And twenty! And *forty*, that is, with the twenty he made on the course."

"It's amazing!" said the uncle.

"If Master Paul offers you to be partners, sir, I would if I were you: if you'll excuse me," said Bassett.

Oscar Cresswell thought about it.

"I'll see the money," he said.

They drove home again, and, sure enough, Bassett came round to the garden-house with fifteen hundred pounds in notes. The twenty pounds reserve was left with Joe Glee, in the Turf Commission deposit.

"You see, it's all right, uncle, when I'm *sure!* Then we go strong, for all we're worth. Don't we, Bassett?"

"We do that, Master Paul."

"And when are you sure?" said the uncle, laughing.

"Oh, well, sometimes I'm *absolutely* sure, like about Daffodil," said the boy; "and sometimes I have an idea; and sometimes I haven't even an idea, have I, Bassett? Then we're careful, because we mostly go down."

"You do, do you! And when you're sure, like about Daffodil, what makes you sure, sonny?"

"Oh, well, I don't know," said the boy uneasily. "I'm sure, you know, uncle; that's all."

"It's as if he had it from heaven, sir," Bassett reiterated.

"I should say so!" said the uncle.

But he became a partner. And when the Leger was coming on, Paul was "sure" about Lively Spark, which was a quite inconsiderable horse. The boy insisted on putting a thousand on the horse, Bassett went for five hundred, and Oscar Cresswell two hundred. Lively Spark came in first, and the betting had been ten to one against him. Paul had made ten thousand.

"You see," he said, "I was absolutely sure of him."

Even Oscar Cresswell had cleared two thousand.

"Look here, son," he said, "this sort of thing makes me nervous."

"It needn't, uncle! Perhaps I shan't be sure again for a long time."

"But what are you going to do with your money?" asked the uncle.

"Of course," said the boy, "I started it for mother. She said she had no luck, because father is unlucky, so I thought if *I* was lucky, it might stop whispering."

"What might stop whispering?"

"Our house. I *hate* our house for whispering."

"What does it whisper?"

"Why – why" – the boy fidgeted – "why, I don't know! But it's always short of money, you know, uncle."

"I know it, son, I know it."

"You know people send mother writs, don't you, uncle?"

"I'm afraid I do," said the uncle.

"And then the house whispers, like people laughing at you behind your back. It's awful, that is! I thought if I was lucky—"

"You might stop it," added the uncle.

The boy watched him with big blue eyes, that had an uncanny cold fire in them, and he never said a word.

"Well, then!" said the uncle. "What are we doing?"

"I shouldn't like mother to know I was lucky," said the boy.

"Why not, son?"

"She'd stop me."

"I don't think she would."

"Oh!" – and the boy writhed in an odd way – "I *don't* want her to know, uncle."

"All right, son! We'll manage it without her knowing."

They managed it very easily. Paul, at the other's suggestion, handed over five thousand pounds to his uncle, who deposited it with the family lawyer, who was then to inform Paul's mother that a relative had put five thousand pounds into his hands, which sum was to be paid out a thousand pounds at a time, on the mother's birthday, for the next five years.

"So she'll have a birthday present of a thousand pounds for five successive years," said Uncle Oscar. "I hope it won't make it all the harder for her later."

Paul's mother had her birthday in November. The house had been "whispering" worse than ever lately; and, even in spite of his luck, Paul could not bear up against it. He was very anxious to see the effect of the birthday letter, telling his mother about the thousand pounds.

When there were no visitors, Paul now took his meals with his parents, as he was beyond the nursery control. His mother went into town nearly every day. She had discovered that she had an odd knack of sketching furs and dress materials, so she worked secretly in the studio of a friend who was the chief "artist" for the leading drapers. She drew the figures of ladies in furs and ladies in silk and sequins for the newspaper advertisements. This young woman artist earned several thousand pounds a year, but Paul's mother only made several hundreds, and she was again dissatisfied. She so wanted to be first in something, and she did not succeed, even in making sketches for drapery advertisements.

She was down to breakfast on the morning of her birthday. Paul watched her face as she read her letters. He knew the lawyer's letter. As his mother read it, her face hardened and became more expressionless. Then a cold, determined look came on her mouth. She hid the letter under the pile of others, and said not a word about it.

"Didn't you have anything nice in the post for your birthday, mother?" said Paul.

"Quite moderately nice," she said, her voice cold and absent.

She went away to town without saying more.

But in the afternoon Uncle Oscar appeared. He said Paul's mother had had a long interview with the lawyer, asking if the whole five thousand could not be advanced at once, as she was in debt.

"What do you think, uncle?" said the boy.

"I leave it to you, son."

"Oh, let her have it, then! We can get some more with the other," said the boy.

"A bird in the hand is worth two in the bush, laddie!" said Uncle Oscar.

"But I'm sure to *know* for the Grand National; or the Lincolnshire; or else the Derby. I'm sure to know for *one* of them," said Paul.

So Uncle Oscar signed the agreement, and Paul's mother touched the whole five thousand. Then something very curious happened. The voices in the house suddenly went mad, like a chorus of frogs on a spring evening. There were certain new furnishings, and Paul had a tutor. He was *really* going to Eton, his father's school, in the following autumn. There were flowers in the winter, and a blossoming of the luxury Paul's mother had been used to. And yet the voices in the house, behind the sprays of mimosa and almond-blossom, and from under the piles of iridescent cushions, simply trilled and screamed in a sort of ecstasy: "There *must* be more money! Oh-h-h! There *must* be more money! Oh, now, now-w! Now-w-w – there *must* be more money! – more than ever! More than ever!"

It frightened Paul terribly. He studied away at his Latin and Greek with his tutor. But his intense hours were spent with Bassett. The Grand National had gone by: he had not "known", and had lost a hundred pounds. Summer was at hand. He was in agony for the Lincoln. But even for the Lincoln he didn't "know", and he lost fifty pounds. He became wild-eyed and strange, as if something were going to explode in him.

"Let it alone, son! Don't you bother about it!" urged Uncle Oscar. But it was as if the boy couldn't really hear what his uncle was saying.

"I've got to know for the Derby! I've *got* to know for the Derby!" the child reiterated, his big blue eyes blazing with a sort of madness.

His mother noticed how overwrought he was.

"You'd better go to the seaside. Wouldn't you like to go now to the seaside, instead of waiting? I think you'd better," she said, looking down at him anxiously, her heart curiously heavy because of him.

But the child lifted his uncanny blue eyes.

"I couldn't possibly go before the Derby, mother!" he said. "I couldn't possibly!"

"Why not?" she said, her voice becoming heavy when she was opposed. "Why not? You can still go from the seaside to see the Derby with your Uncle Oscar, if that's what you wish. No need for you to wait here. Besides, I think you care too much about these races. It's a bad sign. My family has been a gambling family, and you won't know till you grow up how much damage it has done. But it has done damage. I shall have to send Bassett away, and ask Uncle Oscar not to talk racing to you, unless you promise to be reasonable about it: go away to the seaside and forget it. You're all nerves!"

"I'll do what you like, mother, so long as you don't send me away till after the Derby," the boy said.

"Send you away from where? Just from this house?"

"Yes," he said, gazing at her.

"Why, you curious child, what makes you care about this house so much, suddenly? I never knew you loved it!"

He gazed at her without speaking. He had a secret within a secret, something he had not divulged, even to Bassett or to his Uncle Oscar.

But his mother, after standing undecided and a little bit sullen for some moments, said:

"Very well, then! Don't go to the seaside till after the Derby, if you don't wish it. But promise me you won't let your nerves go to pieces. Promise you won't think so much about horse-racing and *events*, as you call them!"

"Oh no," said the boy casually. "I won't think much about them, mother. You needn't worry. I wouldn't worry, mother, if I were you."

"If you were me and I were you," said his mother, "I wonder what we *should* do!"

"But you know you needn't worry, mother, don't you?" the boy repeated.

"I should be awfully glad to know it," she said wearily.

"Oh, well, you *can*, you know. I mean, you *ought* to know you needn't worry," he insisted.

"Ought I? Then I'll see about it," she said.

Paul's secret of secrets was his wooden horse, that which had no name. Since he was emancipated from a nurse and a nursery governess, he had had his rocking-horse removed to his own bedroom at the top of the house.

"Surely you're too big for a rocking-horse!" his mother had remonstrated.

"Well, you see, mother, till I can have a *real* horse, I like to have *some* sort of animal about," had been his quaint answer.

"Do you feel he keeps you company?" she laughed.

"Oh yes! He's very good; he always keeps me company, when I'm there," said Paul.

So the horse, rather shabby, stood in an arrested prance in the boy's bedroom.

The Derby was drawing near, and the boy grew more and more tense. He hardly heard what was spoken to him, he was very frail, and his eyes were really uncanny. His mother had sudden seizures of uneasiness about him. Sometimes, for half an hour, she would feel a sudden anxiety about him that was almost anguish. She wanted to rush to him at once, and know he was safe.

Two nights before the Derby, she was at a big party in town, when one of her rushes of anxiety about her boy, her first-born, gripped her heart till she could hardly speak. She fought with the feeling, might and main, for she believed in common sense. But it was too strong. She had to leave the dance and go downstairs to telephone to the country.

The children's nursery governess was terribly surprised and startled at being rung up in the night.

"Are the children all right, Miss Wilmot?"

"Oh yes, they are quite all right."

"Master Paul? Is he all right?"

"He went to bed as right as a trivet. Shall I run up and look at him?"

"No," said Paul's mother reluctantly. "No! Don't trouble. It's all right. Don't sit up. We shall be home fairly soon." She did not want her son's privacy intruded upon.

"Very good," said the governess.

It was about one o'clock when Paul's mother and father drove up to their house. All was still. Paul's mother went to her room and slipped off her white fur cloak. She had told her maid not to wait up for her. She heard her husband downstairs mixing a whisky and soda.

And then, because of the strange anxiety at her heart, she stole upstairs to her son's room. Noiselessly she went along the upper corridor. Was there a faint noise? What was it?

She stood, with arrested muscles, outside his door, listening. There was a strange, heavy, and yet not loud noise. Her heart stood still. It was a soundless noise, yet rushing and powerful. Something huge, in violent, hushed motion. What was it? What in God's name was it? She ought to know. She felt that she *knew* the noise. She knew what it was.

Yet she could not place it. She couldn't say what it was. And on and on it went, like a madness.

Softly, frozen with anxiety and fear, she turned the door-handle.

The room was dark. Yet in the space near the window, she heard and saw something plunging to and fro. She gazed in fear and amazement.

Then suddenly she switched on the light, and saw her son, in his green pyjamas, madly surging on the rocking-horse. The blaze of light suddenly lit him up, as he urged the wooden horse, and lit her up, as she stood, blonde, in her dress of pale green and crystal, in the doorway.

"Paul!" she cried. "Whatever are you doing?"

"It's Malabar!" he screamed in a powerful, strange voice. "It's Malabar!"

His eyes blazed at her for one strange and senseless second, as he ceased urging his wooden horse. Then he fell with a crash to the ground, and she, all her tormented motherhood flooding upon her, rushed to gather him up.

But he was unconscious, and unconscious he remained, with some brain-fever. He talked and tossed, and his mother sat stonily by his side.

"Malabar! It's Malabar! Bassett, Bassett, I know! It's Malabar!"

So the child cried, trying to get up and urge the rocking-horse that gave him his inspiration.

"What does he mean by Malabar?" asked the heart-frozen mother.

"I don't know," said the father stonily.

"What does he mean by Malabar?" she asked her brother Oscar.

"It's one of the horses running for the Derby," was the answer.

And, in spite of himself, Oscar Cresswell spoke to Bassett, and himself put a thousand on Malabar: at fourteen to one.

The third day of the illness was critical: they were watching for a change. The boy, with his rather long, curly hair, was tossing ceaselessly on the pillow. He neither slept nor regained consciousness, and his eyes were like blue stones. His mother sat, feeling her heart had gone, turned actually into a stone.

In the evening, Oscar Cresswell did not come, but Bassett sent a message, saying could he come up for one moment, just one moment? Paul's mother was very angry at the intrusion, but on second thoughts she agreed. The boy was the same. Perhaps Bassett might bring him to consciousness.

The gardener, a shortish fellow with a little brown moustache and sharp little brown eyes, tiptoed into the room, touched his imaginary cap to Paul's mother, and stole to the bedside, staring with glittering, smallish eyes at the tossing, dying child.

"Master Paul!" he whispered. "Master Paul! Malabar came in first all right, a clean win. I did as you told me. You've made over seventy thousand pounds, you have; you've got over eighty thousand. Malabar came in all right, Master Paul."

"Malabar! Malabar! Did I say Malabar, mother? Did I say Malabar? Do you think I'm lucky, mother? I knew Malabar, didn't I? Over eighty thousand pounds! I call that lucky, don't you, mother? Over eighty thousand pounds! I knew, didn't I know I knew? Malabar came in all right. If I ride my horse till I'm sure, then I tell you, Bassett, you can go as high as you like. Did you go for all you were worth, Bassett?"

"I went a thousand on it, Master Paul."

"I never told you, mother, that if I can ride my horse, and *get there*, then I'm absolutely sure – oh, absolutely! Mother, did I ever tell you? I *am* lucky!"

"No, you never did," said his mother.

But the boy died in the night.

And even as he lay dead, his mother heard her brother's voice saying to her: "My God, Hester, you're eighty-odd thousand to the good, and a poor devil of a son to the bad. But, poor devil, poor devil, he's best gone out of a life where he rides his rocking-horse to find a winner."

To Build a Fire

Jack London

Day had broken cold and gray, exceedingly cold and gray, when the man turned aside from the main Yukon trail and climbed the high earth-bank, where a dim and little-travelled trail led eastward through the fat spruce timberland. It was a steep bank, and he paused for breath at the top, excusing the act to himself by looking at his watch. It was nine o'clock. There was no sun nor hint of sun, though there was not a cloud in the sky. It was a clear day, and yet there seemed an intangible pall over the face of things, a subtle gloom that made the day dark, and that was due to the absence of sun. This fact did not worry the man. He was used to the lack of sun. It had been days since he had seen the sun, and he knew that a few more days must pass before that cheerful orb, due south, would just peep above the sky-line and dip immediately from view.

The man flung a look back along the way he had come. The Yukon lay a mile wide and hidden under three feet of ice. On top of this ice were as many feet of snow. It was all pure white, rolling in gentle undulations where the ice-jams of the freeze-up had formed. North and south, as far as his eye could see, it was unbroken white, save for a dark hair-line that curved and twisted from around the spruce-covered island to the south, and that curved and twisted away into the north, where it disappeared behind another spruce-covered island. This dark hair-line was the trail – the main trail – that led south five hundred miles to the Chilcoot Pass, Dyea, and salt water; and that led north seventy miles to Dawson, and still on to the north a thousand miles to Nulato, and finally to St. Michael on Bering Sea, a thousand miles and half a thousand more.

But all this – the mysterious, far-reaching hair-line trail, the absence of sun from the sky, the tremendous cold, and the strangeness and weirdness of it all – made no impression on the man. It was not because he was long used to it. He was a newcomer in the land, a *chechaquo*, and this was his first winter. The trouble with him was that he was without imagination. He was quick and alert in the things of life, but only in the things, and not in the significances. Fifty degrees below zero meant eighty-odd degrees of frost. Such fact impressed him as being cold and uncomfortable, and that was all. It did not lead him to meditate upon his frailty as a creature of temperature, and upon man's frailty in general, able only to live within certain narrow limits of heat and cold; and from there on it did not lead him to the conjectural field of immortality and man's place in the universe. Fifty degrees below zero stood for a bite of frost that hurt and that must be guarded against by the use of mittens, ear-flaps, warm moccasins, and thick socks. Fifty degrees below zero was to him just precisely fifty degrees below zero. That there should be anything more to it than that was a thought that never entered his head.

As he turned to go on, he spat speculatively. There was a sharp, explosive crackle that startled him. He spat again. And again, in the air, before it could fall to the snow, the spittle crackled. He knew that at fifty below spittle crackled on the snow, but this spittle had crackled in the air. Undoubtedly it was colder than fifty below — how much colder he did not know. But the temperature did not matter. He was bound for the old claim on the left fork of Henderson Creek, where the boys were already. They had come over across the divide from the Indian Creek country, while he had come the roundabout way to take a look at the possibilities of getting out logs in the spring from the islands in the Yukon. He would be in to camp by six o'clock; a bit after dark, it was true, but the boys would be there, a fire would be going, and a hot supper would be ready. As for lunch, he pressed his hand against the protruding bundle under his jacket. It was also under his shirt, wrapped up in a handkerchief and lying against the naked skin. It was the only way to keep the biscuits from freezing. He smiled agreeably to himself as he thought of those biscuits, each cut open and sopped in bacon grease, and each enclosing a generous slice of fried bacon.

He plunged in among the big spruce trees. The trail was faint. A foot of snow had fallen since the last sled had passed over, and he was glad he was without a sled, travelling light. In fact, he carried nothing but the lunch wrapped in the handkerchief. He was surprised, however, at the cold. It certainly was cold, he concluded, as he rubbed his numb nose and cheek-bones with his mittened hand. He was a warm-whiskered man, but the hair on his face did not protect the high cheek-bones and the eager nose that thrust itself aggressively into the frosty air.

At the man's heels trotted a dog, a big native husky, the proper wolf-dog, gray-coated and without any visible or temperamental difference from its brother, the wild wolf. The animal was depressed by the tremendous cold. It knew that it was no time for travelling. Its instinct told it a truer tale than was told to the man by the man's judgment. In reality, it was not merely colder than fifty below zero; it was colder than sixty below, than seventy below. It was seventy-five below zero. Since the freezing-point is thirty-two above zero, it meant that one hundred and seven degrees of frost obtained. The dog did not know anything about thermometers. Possibly in its brain there was no sharp consciousness of a condition of very cold such as was in the man's brain. But the brute had its instinct. It experienced a vague but menacing apprehension that subdued it and made it slink along at the man's heels, and that made it question eagerly every unwonted movement of the man as if expecting him to go into camp or to seek shelter somewhere and build a fire. The dog had learned fire, and it wanted fire, or else to burrow under the snow and cuddle its warmth away from the air.

The frozen moisture of its breathing had settled on its fur in a fine powder of frost, and especially were its jowls, muzzle, and eyelashes whitened by its crystalled breath. The man's red beard and mustache were likewise frosted, but more solidly, the deposit taking the form of ice and increasing with every warm, moist breath he exhaled. Also, the man was chewing tobacco, and the muzzle of ice held his lips so rigidly that he was unable to clear his chin when he expelled the juice. The result was that a crystal beard of the color and solidity of amber was increasing its length on his chin. If he fell down it would shatter itself, like glass, into brittle fragments. But he did not mind the appendage. It was the penalty all tobacco-chewers paid in that country, and he had been out before in two cold snaps. They had not been so cold as this, he knew, but by the spirit thermometer at Sixty Mile he knew they had been registered at fifty below and at fifty-five.

He held on through the level stretch of woods for several miles, crossed a wide flat of niggerheads, and dropped down a bank to the frozen bed of a small stream. This was Henderson Creek, and he knew he was ten miles from the forks. He looked at his watch. It was ten o'clock. He was making four miles an hour, and he calculated that he would arrive at the forks at half-past twelve. He decided to celebrate that event by eating his lunch there.

The dog dropped in again at his heels, with a tail drooping discouragement, as the man swung along the creek-bed. The furrow of the old sled-trail was plainly visible, but a dozen inches of snow covered the marks of the last runners. In a month no man had come up or down that silent creek. The man held steadily on. He was not much given to thinking, and just then particularly he had nothing to think about save that he would eat lunch at the forks and that at six o'clock he would be in camp with the boys. There was nobody to talk to; and, had there been, speech would have been impossible because of the ice-muzzle on his mouth. So he continued monotonously to chew tobacco and to increase the length of his amber beard.

Once in a while the thought reiterated itself that it was very cold and that he had never experienced such cold. As he walked along he rubbed his cheek-bones and nose with the back of his mittened hand. He did this automatically, now and again changing hands. But rub as he would, the instant he stopped his cheek-bones went numb, and the following instant the end of his nose went numb. He was sure to frost his cheeks; he knew that, and experienced a pang of regret that he had not devised a nose-strap of the sort Bud wore in cold snaps. Such a strap passed across the cheeks, as well, and saved them. But it didn't matter much, after all. What were frosted cheeks? A bit painful, that was all; they were never serious.

Empty as the man's mind was of thoughts, he was keenly observant, and he noticed the changes in the creek, the curves and bends and timber-jams, and always he sharply noted where he placed his feet. Once, coming around a bend, he shied abruptly, like a startled horse, curved away from the place where he had been walking, and retreated several paces back along the trail. The creek he knew was frozen clear to the bottom – no creek could contain water in that arctic winter – but he knew also that there were springs that bubbled out from the hillsides and ran along under the snow and on top the ice of the creek. He knew that the coldest snaps never froze these springs, and he knew likewise their danger. They were traps. They hid pools of water under the snow that might be three inches deep, or three feet.

Sometimes a skin of ice half an inch thick covered them, and in turn was covered by the snow. Sometimes there were alternate layers of water and ice-skin, so that when one broke through he kept on breaking through for a while, sometimes wetting himself to the waist.

That was why he had shied in such panic. He had felt the give under his feet and heard the crackle of a snow-hidden ice-skin. And to get his feet wet in such a temperature meant trouble and danger. At the very least it meant delay, for he would be forced to stop and build a fire, and under its protection to bare his feet while he dried his socks and moccasins. He stood and studied the creek-bed and its banks, and decided that the flow of water came from the right. He reflected awhile, rubbing his nose and cheeks, then skirted to the left, stepping gingerly and testing the footing for each step. Once clear of the danger, he took a fresh chew of tobacco and swung along at his four-mile gait.

In the course of the next two hours he came upon several similar traps. Usually the snow above the hidden pools had a sunken, candied appearance that advertised the danger. Once again, however, he had a close call; and once, suspecting danger, he compelled the dog to go on in front. The dog did not want to go. It hung back until the man shoved it forward, and then it went quickly across the white, unbroken surface. Suddenly it broke through, floundered to one side, and got away to firmer footing. It had wet its forefeet and legs, and almost immediately the water that clung to it turned to ice. It made quick efforts to lick the ice off its legs, then dropped down in the snow and began to bite out the ice that had formed between the toes. This was a matter of instinct. To permit the ice to remain would mean sore feet. It did not know this. It merely obeyed the mysterious prompting that arose from the deep crypts of its being. But the man knew, having achieved a judgment on the subject, and he removed the mitten from his right hand and helped tear out the ice-particles. He did not expose his fingers more than a minute, and was astonished at the swift numbness that smote them. It certainly was cold. He pulled on the mitten hastily, and beat the hand savagely across his chest.

At twelve o'clock the day was at its brightest. Yet the sun was too far south on its winter journey to clear the horizon. The bulge of the earth intervened between it and Henderson Creek, where the man walked under a clear sky at noon and cast no shadow. At half-past twelve, to the minute, he arrived at the forks of the creek. He was pleased at the speed he had made. If he kept it up, he would certainly be with the boys by six. He unbuttoned his jacket and shirt and drew forth his lunch. The action consumed no more than a quarter of a minute, yet in that brief moment the numbness laid hold of the exposed fingers. He did not put the mitten on, but, instead, struck the fingers a dozen sharp smashes against his leg. Then he sat down on a snow-covered log to eat. The sting that followed upon the striking of his fingers against his leg ceased so quickly that he was startled. He had had no chance to take a bite of biscuit. He struck the fingers repeatedly and returned them to the mitten, baring the other hand for the purpose of eating. He tried to take a mouthful, but the ice-muzzle prevented. He had forgotten to build a fire and thaw out. He chuckled at his foolishness, and as he chuckled he noted the numbness creeping into the exposed fingers. Also, he noted that the stinging which had first come to his toes when he sat down was already passing away. He wondered whether the toes were warm or numb. He moved them inside the moccasins and decided that they were numb.

He pulled the mitten on hurriedly and stood up. He was a bit frightened. He stamped up and down until the stinging returned into the feet. It certainly was cold, was his thought. That man from Sulphur Creek had spoken the truth when telling how cold it sometimes got in the country. And he had laughed at him at the time! That showed one must not be too sure of things. There was no mistake about it: it *was* cold. He strode up and down, stamping his feet and threshing his arms, until reassured by the returning warmth. Then he got out matches and proceeded to make a fire. From the under-growth, where high water of the previous spring had lodged a supply of seasoned twigs, he got his fire-wood. Working carefully from a small beginning, he soon had a roaring fire, over which he thawed the ice from his face and in the pro-tection of which he ate his biscuits. For the moment the cold of space was outwitted. The dog took satisfaction in the fire, stretching out close enough for warmth and far enough away to escape being singed.

When the man had finished, he filled his pipe and took his comfortable time over a smoke. Then he pulled on his mittens, settled the ear-flaps of his cap firmly about his ears, and took the creek trail up the left fork. The dog was disappointed and yearned back toward the fire. This man did not know cold. Possibly all the generations of his ancestry had been ignorant of cold, of real cold, of cold one hundred and seven degrees below freezing-point. But the dog knew; all its ancestry knew, and it had inherited the knowledge. And it knew that it was not good to walk abroad in such fearful cold. It was the time to lie snug in a hole in the snow and wait for a curtain of cloud to be drawn across the face of outer space whence this cold came. On the other hand, there was no keen intimacy between the dog and the man. The one was the toil-slave of the other, and the only caresses it had ever received were the caresses of the whip-lash and of harsh and menacing throat-sounds that threatened the whip-lash. So the dog made no effort to communicate its apprehension to the man. It was not concerned in the welfare of the man; it was for its own sake that it yearned back toward the fire. But the man whistled, and spoke to it with the sound of whip-lashes, and the dog swung in at the man's heels and followed after.

The man took a chew of tobacco and proceeded to start a new amber beard. Also, his moist breath quickly powdered with white his mustache, eyebrows, and lashes. There did not seem to be so many springs on the left fork of the Henderson, and for half an hour the man saw no signs of any. And then it happened. At a place where there were no signs, where the soft, unbroken snow seemed to advertise solidity beneath, the man broke through. It was not deep. He wet himself halfway to the knees before he floundered out to the firm crust.

He was angry, and cursed his luck aloud. He had hoped to get into camp with the boys at six o'clock, and this would delay him an hour, for he would have to build a fire and dry out his foot-gear. This was imperative at that low temperature – he knew that much; and he turned aside to the bank, which he climbed. On top, tangled in the underbrush about the trunks of several small spruce trees, was a high-water deposit of dry fire-wood – sticks and twigs, principally, but also larger portions of seasoned branches and fine, dry, last-year's grasses. He threw down several large pieces on top of the snow. This served for a foundation and prevented the young flame from drowning itself in the snow it otherwise would melt. The flame he got by touching a match to a small shred of birch-bark that he took from his pocket. This burned even more readily than paper. Placing it on the foundation, he fed the young flame with wisps of dry grass and with the tiniest dry twigs.

He worked slowly and carefully, keenly aware of his danger. Gradually, as the flame grew stronger, he increased the size of the twigs with which he fed it. He squatted in the snow, pulling the twigs out from their entanglement in the brush and feeding directly to the flame. He knew there must be no failure. When it is seventy-five below zero, a man must not fail in his first attempt to build a fire – that is, if his feet are wet. If his feet are dry, and he fails, he can run along the trail for half a mile and restore his circulation. But the circulation of wet and freezing feet cannot be restored by running when it is seventy-five below. No matter how fast he runs, the wet feet will freeze the harder.

All this the man knew. The old-timer on Sulphur Creek had told him about it the previous fall, and now he was appreciating the advice. Already all sensation had gone out of his feet. To build the fire he had been forced to remove his mittens, and the fingers had quickly gone numb. His pace of four miles an hour had kept his heart pumping blood to the surface of his body and to all the extremities. But the instant he stopped, the action of the pump eased down. The cold of space smote the unprotected tip of the planet, and he, being on that unprotected tip, received the full force of the blow. The blood of his body recoiled before it. The blood was alive, like the dog, and like the dog it wanted to hide away and cover itself up from the fearful cold. So long as he walked four miles an hour, he pumped that blood, willy-nilly, to the surface; but now it ebbed away and sank down into the recesses of his body. The extremities were the first to feel its absence. His wet feet froze the faster, and his exposed fingers numbed the faster, though they had not yet begun to freeze. Nose and cheeks were already freezing, while the skin of all his body chilled as it lost its blood.

But he was safe. Toes and nose and cheeks would be only touched by the frost, for the fire was beginning to burn with strength. He was feeding it with twigs the size of his finger. In another minute he would be able to feed it with branches the size of his wrist, and then he could remove his wet foot-gear, and, while it dried, he could keep his naked feet warm by the fire, rubbing them at first, of course, with snow. The fire was a success. He was safe. He remembered the advice of the old-timer on Sulphur Creek, and smiled. The old-timer had been very serious in laying down the law that no man must travel alone in the Klondike after fifty below. Well, here he was; he had had the accident; he was alone; and he had saved himself. Those old-timers were rather womanish, some of them, he thought. All a man had to do was to keep his head, and he was all right. Any man who was a man could travel alone. But it was surprising, the rapidity with which his cheeks and nose were freezing. And he had not thought his fingers could go lifeless in so short a time. Lifeless they were, for he could scarcely make them move together to grip a twig, and they seemed remote from his body and from him. When he touched a twig, he had to look and see whether or not he had hold of it. The wires were pretty well down between him and his finger-ends.

All of which counted for little. There was the fire, snapping and crackling and promising life with every dancing flame. He started to untie his moccasins. They were coated with ice; the thick German socks were like sheaths of iron halfway to the knees; and the moccasin strings were like rods of steel all twisted and knotted as by some conflagration. For a moment he tugged with his numb fingers, then, realizing the folly of it, he drew his sheath-knife.

But before he could cut the strings, it happened. It was his own fault or, rather, his mistake. He should not have built the fire under the spruce tree. He should have built it in the open. But it had been easier to pull the twigs from the brush and drop them directly on the fire. Now the tree under which he had done this carried a weight of snow on its boughs. No wind had blown for weeks, and each bough was fully freighted. Each time he had pulled a twig he had communicated a slight agitation to the tree — an imperceptible agitation, so far as he was concerned, but an agitation sufficient to bring about the disaster. High up in the tree one bough capsized its load of snow. This fell on the boughs beneath, capsizing them. This process continued, spreading out and involving the whole tree. It grew like an avalanche, and it descended without warning upon the man and the fire, and the fire was blotted out! Where it had burned was a mantle of fresh and disordered snow.

The man was shocked. It was as though he had just heard his own sentence of death. For a moment he sat and stared at the spot where the fire had been. Then he grew very calm. Perhaps the old-timer on Sulphur Creek was right. If he had only had a trail-mate he would have been in no danger now. The trail-mate could have built the fire. Well, it was up to him to build the fire over again, and this second time there must be no failure. Even if he succeeded, he would most likely lose some toes. His feet must be badly frozen by now, and there would be some time before the second fire was ready.

Such were his thoughts, but he did not sit and think them. He was busy all the time they were passing through his mind. He made a new foundation for a fire, this time in the open, where no treacherous tree could blot it out. Next, he gathered dry grasses and tiny twigs from the high-water flotsam. He could not bring his fingers together to pull them out, but he was able to gather them by the handful.

In this way he got many rotten twigs and bits of green moss that were undesirable, but it was the best he could do. He worked methodically, even collecting an armful of the larger branches to be used later when the fire gathered strength. And all the while the dog sat and watched him, a certain yearning wistfulness in its eyes, for it looked upon him as the fire-provider, and the fire was slow in coming.

When all was ready, the man reached in his pocket for a second piece of birch-bark. He knew the bark was there, and, though he could not feel it with his fingers, he could hear its crisp rustling as he fumbled for it. Try as he would, he could not clutch hold of it. And all the time, in his consciousness, was the knowledge that each instant his feet were freezing. This thought tended to put him in a panic, but he fought against it and kept calm. He pulled on his mittens with his teeth, and threshed his arms back and forth, beating his hands with all his might against his sides. He did this sitting down, and he stood up to do it; and all the while the dog sat in the snow, its wolf-brush of a tail curled around warmly over its forefeet, its sharp wolf-ears pricked forward intently as it watched the man. And the man, as he beat and threshed with his arms and hands, felt a great surge of envy as he regarded the creature that was warm and secure in its natural covering.

After a time he was aware of the first faraway signals of sensation in his beaten fingers. The faint tingling grew stronger till it evolved into a stinging ache that was excruciating, but which the man hailed with satisfaction. He stripped the mitten from his right hand and fetched forth the birch-bark. The exposed fingers were quickly going numb again. Next he brought out his bunch of sulphur matches. But the tremendous cold had already driven the life out of his fingers. In his effort to separate one match from the others, the whole bunch fell in the snow. He tried to pick it out of the snow, but failed. The dead fingers could neither touch nor clutch. He was very careful. He drove the thought of his freezing feet, and nose, and cheeks, out of his mind, devoting his whole soul to the matches. He watched, using the sense of vision in place of that of touch, and when he saw his fingers on each side the bunch, he closed them – that is, he willed to close them, for the wires were down, and the fingers did not obey. He pulled the mitten on the right hand, and beat it fiercely against his knee. Then, with both mittened hands, he scooped the bunch of matches, along with much snow, into his lap. Yet he was no better off.

After some manipulation he managed to get the bunch between the heels of his mittened hands. In this fashion he carried it to his mouth. The ice crackled and snapped when by a violent effort he opened his mouth. He drew the lower jaw in, curled the upper lip out of the way, and scraped the bunch with his upper teeth in order to separate a match. He succeeded in getting one, which he dropped on his lap. He was no better off. He could not pick it up. Then he devised a way. He picked it up in his teeth and scratched it on his leg. Twenty times he scratched before he succeeded in lighting it. As it flamed he held it with his teeth to the birch-bark. But the burning brimstone went up his nostrils and into his lungs, causing him to cough spasmodically. The match fell into the snow and went out.

The old-timer on Sulphur Creek was right, he thought in the moment of controlled despair that ensued: after fifty below, a man should travel with a partner. He beat his hands, but failed in exciting any sensation. Suddenly he bared both hands, removing the mittens with his teeth. He caught the whole bunch between the heels of his hands. His arm-muscles not being frozen enabled him to press the hand-heels tightly against the matches. Then he scratched the bunch along his leg. It flared into flame, seventy sulphur matches at once! There was no wind to blow them out. He kept his head to one side to escape the strangling fumes, and held the blazing bunch to the birch-bark. As he so held it, he became aware of sensation in his hand. His flesh was burning. He could smell it. Deep down below the surface he could feel it. The sensation developed into pain that grew acute. And still he endured it, holding the flame of the matches clumsily to the bark that would not light readily because his own burning hands were in the way, absorbing most of the flame.

At last, when he could endure no more, he jerked his hands apart. The blazing matches fell sizzling into the snow, but the birch-bark was alight. He began laying dry grasses and the tiniest twigs on the flame. He could not pick and choose, for he had to lift the fuel between the heels of his hands. Small pieces of rotten wood and green moss clung to the twigs, and he bit them off as well as he could with his teeth. He cherished the flame carefully and awkwardly. It meant life, and it must not perish. The withdrawal of blood from the surface of his body now made him begin to shiver, and he grew more awkward. A large piece of green moss fell squarely on the little fire. He tried to poke it out with his fingers, but his shivering frame made him poke too far, and he disrupted the nucleus of the little fire, the burning grasses and tiny twigs separating and scattering. He tried to poke them together again, but in spite of the tenseness of the effort, his shivering got away with him, and the twigs were hopelessly scattered. Each twig gushed a puff of smoke and went out. The fire-provider had failed. As he looked apathetically about him, his eyes chanced on the dog, sitting across the ruins of the fire from him, in the snow, making restless, hunching movements, slightly lifting one forefoot and then the other, shifting its weight back and forth on them with wistful eagerness.

The sight of the dog put a wild idea into his head. He remembered the tale of the man, caught in a blizzard, who killed a steer and crawled inside the carcass, and so was saved. He would kill the dog and bury his hands in the warm body until the numbness went out of them. Then he could build another fire. He spoke to the dog, calling it to him, but in his voice was a strange note of fear that frightened the animal, who had never known the man to speak in such a way before. Something was the matter, and its suspicious nature sensed danger – it knew not what danger, but somewhere, somehow, in its brain arose an apprehension of the man. It flattened its ears down at the sound of the man's voice, and its restless, hunching movements and the liftings and shiftings of its forefeet became more pronounced, but it would not come to the man. He got on his hands and knees and crawled toward the dog. This unusual posture again excited suspicion, and the animal sidled mincingly away.

The man sat up in the snow for a moment and struggled for calmness. Then he pulled on his mittens, by means of his teeth, and got upon his feet. He glanced down at first in order to assure himself that he was really standing up, for the absence of sensation in his feet left him unrelated to the earth. His erect position in itself started to drive the webs of suspicion from the dog's mind; and when he spoke peremptorily, with the sound of whip-lashes in his voice, the dog rendered its customary allegiance and came to him. As it came within reaching distance, the man lost his control. His arms flashed out to the dog, and he experienced genuine surprise when he discovered that his hands could not clutch, that there was neither bend nor feeling in the fingers. He had forgotten for the moment that they were frozen and that they were freezing more and more. All this happened quickly, and before the animal could get away, he encircled its body with his arms. He sat down in the snow, and in this fashion held the dog, while it snarled and whined and struggled.

But it was all he could do, hold its body encircled in his arms and sit there. He realized that he could not kill the dog. There was no way to do it. With his helpless hands he could neither draw nor hold his sheath-knife nor throttle the animal. He released it, and it plunged wildly away, with tail between its legs, and still snarling. It halted forty feet away and surveyed him curiously, with ears sharply pricked forward. The man looked down at his hands in order to locate them, and found them hanging on the ends of his arms. It struck him as curious that one should have to use his eyes in order to find out where his hands were. He began threshing his arms back and forth, beating the mittened hands against his sides. He did this for five minutes, violently, and his heart pumped enough blood up to the surface to put a stop to his shivering. But no sensation was aroused in the hands. He had an impression that they hung like weights on the ends of his arms, but when he tried to run the impression down, he could not find it.

A certain fear of death, dull and oppressive, came to him. This fear quickly became poignant as he realized that it was no longer a mere matter of freezing his fingers and toes, or of losing his hands and feet, but that it was a matter of life and death with the chances against him. This threw him into a panic, and he turned and ran up the creek-bed along the old, dim trail. The dog joined in behind and kept up with him. He ran blindly, without intention, in fear such as he had never known in his life. Slowly, as he ploughed and floundered through the snow, he began to see things again – the banks of the creek, the old timber-jams, the leafless aspens, and the sky. The running made him feel better. He did not shiver. Maybe, if he ran on, his feet would thaw out; and, anyway, if he ran far enough, he would reach camp and the boys. Without doubt he would lose some fingers and toes and some of his face; but the boys would take care of him, and save the rest of him when he got there. And at the same time there was another thought in his mind that said he would never get to the camp and the boys; that it was too many miles away, that the freezing had too great a start on him, and that he would soon be stiff and dead. This thought he kept in the background and refused to consider. Sometimes it pushed itself forward and demanded to be heard, but he thrust it back and strove to think of other things.

It struck him as curious that he could run at all on feet so frozen that he could not feel them when they struck the earth and took the weight of his body. He seemed to himself to skim along above the surface, and to have no connection with the earth. Somewhere he had once seen a winged Mercury, and he wondered if Mercury felt as he felt when skimming over the earth.

His theory of running until he reached camp and the boys had one flaw in it: he lacked the endurance. Several times he stumbled, and finally he tottered, crumpled up, and fell. When he tried to rise, he failed. He must sit and rest, he decided, and next time he would merely walk and keep on going. As he sat and regained his breath, he noted that he was feeling quite warm and comfortable. He was not shivering, and it even seemed that a warm glow had come to his chest and trunk. And yet, when he touched his nose or cheeks, there was no sensation. Running would not thaw them out. Nor would it thaw out his hands and feet. Then the thought came to him that the frozen portions of his body must be extending. He tried to keep this thought down, to forget it, to think of something else; he was aware of the panicky feeling that it caused, and he was afraid of the panic. But the thought asserted itself, and persisted, until it produced a vision of his body totally frozen. This was too much, and he made another wild run along the trail. Once he slowed down to a walk, but the thought of the freezing extending itself made him run again.

And all the time the dog ran with him, at his heels. When he fell down a second time, it curled its tail over its forefeet and sat in front of him, facing him, curiously eager and intent. The warmth and security of the animal angered him, and he cursed it till it flattened down its ears appeasingly. This time the shivering came more quickly upon the man. He was losing in his battle with the frost. It was creeping into his body from all sides. The thought of it drove him on, but he ran no more than a hundred feet, when he staggered and pitched headlong. It was his last panic. When he had recovered his breath and control, he sat up and entertained in his mind the conception of meeting death with dignity. However, the conception did not come to him in such terms. His idea of it was that he had been making a fool of himself, running around like a chicken with its head cut off – such was the simile that occurred to him. Well, he was bound to freeze anyway, and he might as well take it decently. With this new-found peace of mind came the first glimmerings of drowsiness. A good idea, he thought, to sleep off to death. It was like taking an anaesthetic. Freezing was not so bad as people thought. There were lots worse ways to die.

He pictured the boys finding his body next day. Suddenly he found himself with them, coming along the trail and looking for himself. And, still with them, he came around a turn in the trail and found himself lying in the snow. He did not belong with himself any more, for even then he was out of himself, standing with the boys and looking at himself in the snow. It certainly was cold, was his thought. When he got back to the States he could tell the folks what real cold was. He drifted on from this to a vision of the old-timer on Sulphur Creek. He could see him quite clearly, warm and comfortable, and smoking a pipe.

"You were right, old hoss; you were right," the man mumbled to the old-timer of Sulphur Creek.

Then the man drowsed off into what seemed to him the most comfortable and satisfying sleep he had ever known. The dog sat facing him and waiting. The brief day drew to a close in a long, slow twilight. There were no signs of a fire to be made, and, besides, never in the dog's experience had it known a man to sit like that in the snow and make no fire. As the twilight drew on, its eager yearning for the fire mastered it, and with a great lifting and shifting of forefeet, it whined softly, then flattened its ears down in anticipation of being chidden by the man. But the man remained silent. Later the dog whined loudly. And still later it crept close to the man and caught the scent of death. This made the animal bristle and back away. A little longer it delayed, howling under the stars that leaped and danced and shone brightly in the cold sky. Then it turned and trotted up the trail in the direction of the camp it knew, where were the other food-providers and fire-providers.

At the Airport

Marina Mizzau

Signor Rossi has a serious problem. He is on his way to the airport to meet Signor Bianchi whom he doesn't know and who doesn't know him. On the phone Rossi asked Bianchi, "How will we recognize each other?" and Bianchi answered him, "You won't have a problem recognizing me. I'm really ugly."

Signor Rossi examines a few possible courses of action and then discards them. It's not even worth considering simply introducing himself to Bianchi, assuming he does recognize him, as that would be implicitly agreeing with him about his ugliness. Maybe he could approach Bianchi by saying, "But you aren't that ugly after all; I wouldn't have recognized you." It doesn't take Rossi long, however, to realize how ridiculous this course of action would be; there is an obvious irony in it.

He's now sorry he accepted such an absurd assignment without discussing it in full first. He wishes he had offered a characteristic of his own, out of courtesy if nothing else. "I'm no beauty myself." But this isn't true, really, and Bianchi would feel even worse seeing someone much less ugly than himself describing himself as ugly. And what if Bianchi weren't that ugly after all? Beauty is a subjective thing. Rossi could have said to him on the phone, "You can't possibly be so ugly as to expect me to recognize you by that." But what if he were? That would only make things worse.

The fact remains that he simply can't admit to recognizing him. He could pretend he'd made a mistake. He could stop anyone, perhaps even more than one person, ugly or not so ugly, even somebody good-looking. This would be one way of letting Bianchi know that there was nothing special about his face. But what if this offended him even more? Not even allowing him the right to ugliness?

Fair enough: one has the right to be ugly and to be aware of it, maybe even to be proud of it. But one has to take the consequences; an ugly person can claim to be recognized as such, but cannot expect others to acknowledge his ugliness and go beyond the norms of common courtesy.

Signor Rossi consoles himself. His situation isn't that unique after all. How do they manage to select an actor – or worse still an actress – for an ugly role in a film? They must have to tell them why they've been chosen. Or maybe not, maybe they simply tell them they've got to be made up to look ugly. But why, then, the actor will think, did they choose me when there are so many genuinely ugly people to choose from?

If I do recognize him, thinks Rossi, I won't reveal it outright. I'll put on an expression of complete puzzlement that indicates: "Perhaps it's him, but he's not all that ugly." So Bianchi will pick me out, not because of the recognition of his own ugliness, but because he'll see the doubt in my expression and think, He doesn't recognize me; he's not sure.

Maybe I'm not that ugly after all.

Or maybe Bianchi won't recognize the puzzlement as being about his ugliness, but about whether he should show it or not. That's it, Bianchi will be the one to recognize Rossi from his embarrassment. This is what Bianchi must have intended in the first place.

But why make things so complicated? Why didn't Bianchi give him some mark of recognition other than his ugliness, even a minor feature of no great significance which would have allowed Rossi to reduce the principal sign to secondary importance? "I'm ugly and I've got a moustache. I'm ugly and I'm holding the *Corriere della Sera* in my hand." It would have completely altered the situation and Rossi could have said, "It's you, isn't it? I recognized you by your moustache." The fact that there are other moustaches around, perhaps even on good-looking faces, doesn't matter. It would have been an elegant way out from which they would both have benefited. No, Bianchi must be a sadist. He's probably having a great time thinking how Rossi will behave, foreseeing all his apprehensions. Rossi now wants to punish him by saying, "Hello, it's you; yes, you really are ugly."

When Signor Rossi arrives at the airport he hardly dares look around. His gaze takes in a passenger standing near by. He's a very handsome man. Rossi is troubled by an unpleasant suspicion. Is it him? Is he so brazen as to juggle with opposites, so shameless as to stand there and not give in to the temptation of exacting a compliment by means of surprise? Rossi now feels a growing ill will; he would like to confront this man by saying, most earnestly, "Well, you're not so ugly after all." The handsome man starts walking towards him; Rossi looks around: a very beautiful young woman is coming to meet him.

Rossi is at first slightly ashamed of his unkind thought about Bianchi — even more so now that he's finally spotted him. Yes, he is ugly, but not that ugly. Rossi doesn't need to pretend to be puzzled, as he really is. He's embarrassed, not because he has to make a show of not recognizing Bianchi's ugliness, but because he really is uncertain about whether it's him or not. He would like Signor Bianchi, if it *is* him, to recognize his puzzlement and not confuse it with a feigned puzzlement, or with pretend embarrassment.

Yes, it's definitely Bianchi. He isn't very ugly, but he has the air of somebody who *thinks* he's ugly. This arouses a sudden surge of sympathy in Rossi. He would like to acknowledge Bianchi straight away, so as to convey his understanding; but if that is his aim, perhaps the best thing would be not to recognize him.

Signor Rossi gives up. He lowers his gaze and waits.

Eventually they will be the only two left waiting and thus the problem will be solved.

Children of the Vaults

Vladimir Korolenko

My mother died when I was six. My father, absorbed in his grief, seemed altogether to forget my existence. He would pet my little sister Sonya at times and do what he could to make her happy for she reminded him of Mother. But I – I grew wild like some sapling tree in a neglected field. There was no one to care about me. Nor was there anyone to hamper my freedom.

The little town in which we lived was called Kniazhe-Veno; it was very much like any other small town of the Russian south-west. The town was bounded north and south by broad stretches of water and marshland. Tall reeds grew thickly on the marshland, billowing like the sea in every wind. There was an island in the middle of one of the ponds and on it an ancient castle half fallen to ruin.

I recall the dread I always felt looking over the water to that majestic, decaying building. What gruesome tales were told of it. "On human bones the old castle stands," the towns-folk would whisper. Shuddering, I pictured in my childish imagination thousands of skeletons buried beneath the pond, supporting on upraised bony arms the island and the ancient castle.

At one time the old castle had offered free asylum to all

seekers, whoever they might be. The poorest of the poor were given shelter against foul weather. Bit by bit these poor unfortunates tore at the remains of the ancient building, breaking away floors and ceilings for fuel that they might heat stoves, cook what food they could get and manage somehow to keep body and soul together.

But a day came when dissension arose among these people sheltering in the ruins. Then old Janusz, who lived in the castle, got himself appointed to settle the disputes and it was he who decided who might remain and who must leave the island for ever. For weeks after this decision, like so many moles driven from their burrows, several wretched creatures ran about the island – frightened, pitiful, ashamed, holding their rags about them, attempting again and again to slip in, unnoticed, at one or other of the castle's openings. In the end, however unwillingly, they filed across the bridge, disappearing into the dripping murk of the swiftly gathering evening.

From that time on I saw Janusz and the castle in a different light. Meeting me the next day, he urged me to visit. The son of such estimable parents, he assured me with evident satisfaction, might now approach the castle without hesitation; for he would find within its walls only the most respectable of company. He put his hand eagerly on my shoulder but I tore myself free and ran away, my eyes full of tears. The castle had become hateful to me. I could not forget the brutality with which Janusz and his cronies had driven out their unfortunate neighbours. My heart ached at the memory of those poor wretches left without shelter.

Somehow, it was said, these homeless wanderers found refuge on the hill where the old chapel stood. What sort of shelter human beings might find there, no one could say.

The organizer and leader of this band of unfortunates was one Tiburcy Drab, the most remarkable personality of all those driven from the castle. Tiburcy's origins were veiled in the darkest obscurity. Some say he was the bearer of an aristocratic name which he had so disgraced that he had been forced to go into hiding. There was nothing of the aristocrat, however, in his appearance. He was a tall man with massive, coarse but expressive features, and reddish hair, close-cropped and bristling. His low forehead and somewhat protruding lower jaw had something of the monkey in them. But the eyes that gleamed from under his bushy brows had a grim and stubborn look lit by energy and intelligence.

Tiburcy's hands were rough and calloused and he set down his feet in heavy, peasant fashion. How then could he be of aristocratic origins? But how then to explain his extraordinary learning which nobody could deny? There was not a tavern in all the town in which Tiburcy had not edified the peasants gathered for a drink on market day with whole portions from Cicero and his ilk delivered from the top of a wine barrel. Ukrainian peasant folk are richly gifted with imagination and they read meanings of their own into these impassioned if incomprehensible recitations. Tiburcy's voice would roll out in such mournful tones that the more drunken of his listeners would hang their heads until their forelocks fell over their eyes and mumble sadly, "Ah, but he pulls at your heartstrings, the devil," and tears would run from their eyes down their long drooping moustaches.

Then, when Tiburcy sprang suddenly from the barrel top and broke into ringing laughter, the peasants' sorrowful faces would clear and their hands would dive into their pockets in search of coins. They would ply him with vodka, and coins would shower clinking into his cap.

Tiburcy's amazing erudition gave rise to a new legend: that he had been a serf in some count's household and that he had been sent with the count's son to a Jesuit school. That while the young nobleman idled away his years at school, the young serf had absorbed all his master's lessons.

No one knew either where the children came from who lived with Tiburcy – a boy of eight or nine, tall for his age and well grown, and a little girl of about four. The little girl was only seen once or twice – in Tiburcy's arms. Then she disappeared and no one knew where she might be.

There was some talk of underground vaults on the hill where the old chapel stood. The talk was widely believed. After all, these people had to live somewhere and it was always in the direction of the chapel that they disappeared of an evening – the half-insane old beggar nicknamed the Professor hobbling along, Tiburcy with his energetic stride, and all the other strange, suspicious-looking figures. There was no one in all the town who was brave enough to follow them up the slope.

My father and I

Old Janusz from the castle was always reprimanding me for

being one of Tiburcy's listeners. "You're in bad society," he would tell me. "Such a pity – the son of such estimable parents." Indeed, now that Mother was dead and my father's face had grown so morose, I was seldom to be found at home. Late of a summer evening I would creep in through the orchard, stealthy as a wolf cub, carefully avoiding my father. I would prise open my window, half hidden behind the lilac bushes, and slip into my bedroom.

At the first sign of daylight, when all the household was fast asleep, I would be out of doors again, over the orchard fence and off for the pond where my comrades, just such graceless scamps as myself, would be waiting with their fishing rods. Often I would wander off by myself. I liked to watch the awakening of nature. It was a joy to me to start up a lark still lingering in his nest. The dew would still be dripping from the meadow flowers and the trees in the woods outside the town would make me welcome with a lazy, drowsy whispering.

A "vagabond" everyone called me and "a good-for-nothing scamp". I was so often reproached with the most varied of evil tendencies that in time I myself began to believe these reproaches. My father believed them too and tried at times to teach me better ways. But these attempts were always unsuccessful. Confronted by that stern and gloomy face with the mark of hopeless grief upon it, I would stand there, shifting my weight from one foot to the other and keeping my eyes averted. There were moments when something stirred within me, when I wanted to be taken up onto his knees and pressed to his heart. I would have clung to him then and perhaps we might have wept together – child and stern man – for our common loss. But he would look at me with clouded eyes that seemed to stare over my head into the distance and I would shrink before his gaze, which I could not understand.

Gradually the gulf that parted us grew wider. More and more he came to regard me as a spoiled, vicious child, cold-hearted and selfish. It was his duty to love me but he could find no real love for me in his heart. His sense of duty unfulfilled still further estranged him from me.

From the age of six I knew the desolate pain of loneliness.

Sonya, my sister, was only four. I loved her with all my heart and so did she me. But I was regarded by all as an incorrigible young rogue and this built a high wall between us. Every time I began to play with Sonya in my noisy, lively way, her old nurse, dozing over the feathers she was forever plucking, would come wide awake and at once carry my Sonya off into the house, glaring at me as she went.

I had become hardened to reproaches, and having heard them out in sullen silence I would continue to do as I pleased. I would roam about the town observing everything with childish curiosity. When I had explored every corner of the town to the last of its muddy alleys, my thoughts turned to the chapel on the hill. At first, like some timid creature of the woods, I tried the approaches to the hill from every side – wanting to climb it but afraid to, so bad was its reputation. Stare as I might, however, I saw nothing on the hillside but quiet graves and crumbling old tombs. There was not the slightest sign of human habitation or human activity.

As this was rather a scary expedition to undertake alone – and, besides, I might need help – I recruited three young daredevils, bribed by the promise of delicious apples from our orchard.

I make new friends

We set out from the town soon after dinner and went straight to the hill. It was very quiet and the hush of utter peace hung over the abandoned graveyard. We were alone except for the chattering sparrows and the swallows darting in and out of the chapel windows. The stone of the tombs was carpeted with green and dotted with buttercups, clover and violets. The door of the chapel was securely boarded up and the windows were very high. With the help of my comrades I hoped to reach a window and look in.

"Don't!" one of them cried, seizing my arm, his courage suddenly evaporating.

But another, the eldest of our little army, shouldered him out of the way with a contemptuous "Scaredy-cat!" and stooped willingly to help me. I climbed onto his back and could then easily reach the window frame. It proved strong enough to hold me and I swung up and perched on the sill. But it seemed much further from my window to the floor than to the grass outside. I had the feeling of one peering down into a dark pit, but I didn't stop to think. I took two of our belts, tied them together, looped one end over the windowsill and gave it to my companion to hold. By the other end I swung down into the chapel. I shivered a bit when my feet touched the floor but a glance at the friendly face looking down at me from the window restored my courage.

The first step I took rang loudly through the empty chapel and echoed back from the dark corners. A sudden dread came over me but my friend up above, with breathless curiosity and sympathy, whispered down to me, "Will you go any further?"

"Yes," I answered, whispering too.

But at that moment came a startling interruption. It began with the rattle of falling plaster and up in the gallery something stirred, sending down a shower of dust. A great grey bulk rose heavily with flapping wings from one of the darkest corners. It was a huge owl, awakened by our voices. For an instant it blocked the blue patch of sky shining in at the hole in the roof and the chapel grew dark. The next instant it was gone. But it sent me into a sudden fit of panic. "Pull me up," I cried to my comrade, seizing hold of the belt.

"Don't worry," he said soothingly and braced himself to pull me up. But all at once his face contorted with terror and, with a loud cry, he dropped out of sight outside the window. Instinctively I looked behind me. What I saw inspired astonishment rather than horror. An earthen pot flashed through the air and disappeared under the altar, held by a small child's hand. It is not easy to describe my feeling. I was not in this world at all. From I know not where, I heard the rapid frightened patter of two pairs of running feet.

Time for me had ceased so I cannot say how long it was

before I heard voices whispering under the altar.

"Why doesn't he climb out again?"

"He's scared, can't you see?"

The first voice seemed to belong to a very small child, the second to a boy of about my age. I thought too that I saw dark eyes gleam at me through a crack in the altar. There was a sound of something moving. The altar seemed to rock and then, from under it, a human figure emerged. It was a boy, tall and thin as a reed. His hands were thrust into the pockets of his short tight trousers; his shirt was dirty and his dark curly hair hung uncombed over dark wistful eyes.

Though he had appeared on the scene in so sudden and strange a manner, and though he now came towards me with that air of careless bravado which the boys about our market place assumed when they meant to fight – for all that, I was tremendously relieved by the sight of him. I was still more relieved when a face appeared behind him under the altar, or rather in the trapdoor which the altar screened – a dirty little face, framed by fair hair, with sky-blue eyes that looked out at me with childish curiosity.

I moved forward from the wall and I too thrust my hands into my pockets – to indicate that I was not afraid of my opponent and that I held him more or less in contempt.

We stopped, face to face, and for an instant our eyes met. He looked me silently up and down and then demanded, "What are you doing here?"

"Nothing," I answered. "What do you care?"

He hunched a shoulder, as if about to pull his hand from his pocket and hit out at me.

"I'll show you," he threatened.

"Just you try!" I retorted, puffing up my chest.

It was a critical moment. I stood waiting; but my opponent, still measuring me with his eyes, made no further move.

"I can show you too," I said, but rather more peaceably.

All this while the little girl behind him had been trying to climb out at the trapdoor. Grasping its edges with her tiny hands, she had lifted herself several times but each time had fallen back again. Now, at last, she succeeded and came toddling unsteadily across the chapel. Reaching my opponent, she pressed up close to him, her arms round his waist, and turned to look at me, wondering and a little frightened.

That decided it. Clearly he could not fight with the child clinging to him so. And I, of course, was too generous to take advantage of his handicap.

"What's your name?" he asked me, stroking the little girl's hair.

"Vasya. What's yours?"

"Walek. I know who you are. You live in the house up above the pond. You've got the hugest apples in your orchard!"

"Yes, that's true. They are the best! Would you like some?"

I pulled two apples from my pocket, the wages meant for my friends who had so shamefully deserted me, and offered one to Walek and the other to the little girl. But she only clung closer to Walek, hiding her face against him. He handed the apple to her.

Then turning back to me he asked, "What did you come here for? I don't go poking around in your orchard, do I?"

"Come if you like," I replied hospitably.

My answer seemed to puzzle Walek. He hesitated a moment, then said wistfully, "I'm not fit company for you."

"Why not?" I demanded, upset by his sad tone.

"Your father's the judge."

"Well, so what?" I said. "It's me you'll be playing with, not my father."

Walek shook his head. "Tiburcy wouldn't let me," he said. And, as though the name reminded him of something, he went on hurriedly, "Look, you seem to be a good fellow, but just the same you'd better go home. There'll be trouble if Tiburcy finds you here."

I agreed that I had really best be going. The last rays of sunlight were slipping away and it was a good distance back to town.

We did not go down by the pitted slope that I had climbed. Walek knew a better way that took us through the reeds of a dried-up marsh and across a little stream by a bridge of thin boards, and then straight down to the flat land at the foot of the hill. Here we stopped to say goodbye.

"Will you come again?" the little girl asked.

"Yes," I answered, "I surely will."

"Well, yes," Walek said slowly. "I suppose you could. Only pick a time when our people are down in the town."

"Who do you mean by 'our people'?"

"Why, all of them. Tiburcy and the Professor, and all the rest."

"All right, I'll come when I see them in town. Goodbye."

And I started off. But Walek called after me, "Wait a

minute! Look, you won't tell anybody that you saw us, will you?"

"I won't tell anybody," I said without hesitation.

In the days that followed I was entirely absorbed by my new friends. Going to bed at night and getting up in the morning, I thought of nothing but visiting the hill. I had only one purpose now in loitering about the streets: to make sure that all the members of what Janusz had described as "bad society" were safely in town. If I found Tiburcy orating in his usual haunts and the other shady characters of his company loitering about the market place, I would be off at once, on the run across the marsh and up the hill to the chapel, my pockets stuffed with apples and whatever sweets had come my way, for I saved them all for my new friends.

Walek, undemonstrative by nature, and with grown-up ways that rather awed me, would accept these offerings simply and quietly, generally putting away his share for his sister. But Marusya – she would throw up her little hands, her blue eyes dancing with delight. Her pale cheeks would colour and she would laugh out loud. And her laughter would echo in our hearts, rewarding us for the sweets that we denied ourselves to give to her.

She was a pale, puny child, much like a flower that has never known the sun. Four years old, she could not yet walk properly but tottered along with short uncertain steps, swaying like a blade of grass on her rickety little legs.

I could not help but compare her with my sister. They were about the same age but Sonya was so plump and round and lively. She could run so fast when she was in the mood and she laughed so ringingly. She always wore such pretty dresses and there was always a bright red ribbon in her dark plaits.

My new little friend hardly ever ran and very seldom laughed. When she did laugh, it was like the tiniest of silver bells, not to be heard more than a few steps away. Her dress was old and soiled and she had no ribbon in her plaits. Her hair, though, was far thicker and longer than Sonya's. Walek, to my surprise, was very good at plaiting it and did so for her every morning.

I was active and restless. I brought my usual animation into my play with my new friends. Never, in all likelihood, had the old chapel echoed to such shouts as mine as I tried to draw Walek and Marusya into play. But I was not very successful.

Walek would look from me to Marusya, and once, when I tried to make her run, he said, "Don't, she'll cry."

True enough, when I teased her into running off and when she heard me running after her, she suddenly stopped and turned to face me. Her little arms raised as though in defence, she looked at me helplessly, like a trapped bird, and began to cry.

"You see," Walek said, "she doesn't like to play."

He sat her down in the grass, gathered some flowers and threw them to her. She stopped crying and sat quietly picking over the flowers, whispering to the golden buttercups and lifting the bluebells to her lips. Somewhat subdued, I lay down in the grass near by with Walek.

"What makes her that way?" I asked after a while.

"Afraid to play, you mean?" Walek returned. And he answered in a tone of absolute conviction, "Well, you see, it's all because of the grey stone."

"What grey stone?"

"The grey stone sucks the life out of her," Walek explained. He was lying on his back, looking up at the sky. "That's what Tiburcy says and Tiburcy always knows."

I could make nothing of this explanation but I was impressed by Walek's conviction that Tiburcy "always knows". I turned to look at Marusya. She sat just as Walek had set her down, quietly picking over her flowers. The movements of her thin hands were slow and languid. The blue of her eyes, under long drooping lashes, was deepened by the pallor of her face. Surely something was sucking the life out of this strange little girl who cried when other little girls would laugh. But stone – how could stone suck out life?

This puzzle held more dread for me than all the phantoms of the ancient castle. There was something shapeless, merciless, cruel and hard as stone hanging over this little girl.

Influenced by this feeling, I curbed my animation and tried to adapt myself, like Walek, to Marusya's quiet ways. We would run about picking flowers for her, collecting pretty stones, or catching butterflies. Sometimes we would stretch out on the grass beside her, looking up at the clouds floating high over the ragged chapel roof, and tell her stories, or perhaps simply talk.

As the days passed, these talks strengthened our friendship, which grew steadily although we were so unlike in

118

character. I was lively, restless, impulsive. Walek was sober, restrained, and always with a hint of sadness.

Noticing that he spoke of Tiburcy as he might a comrade his own age, I asked, "Isn't Tiburcy your father?"

"I suppose so," he answered slowly, as though the question had never occurred to him.

"Does he like you?"

"Oh, yes." And this time the answer came far more confidently. "He's always worried about me and, you know, he kisses me too, and cries."

"My father doesn't care for me," I said. "He never kisses me. He's just no good."

"No, no!" Walek exclaimed. "That isn't true. You don't understand. Tiburcy knows better. Tiburcy says the judge is the best man in this whole town. Why, he even decided a case against a count once."

"Yes, that's true. The count was terribly angry. I heard him."

"There! And it's no simple thing to go against a count."

"Why?"

"Why?" Walek paused a moment, thinking. "Well, because a count isn't just anybody. A count does whatever he pleases, and rides in a carriage, and a – a count has money. He can give a judge money, and some judges would take his money and decide the case his way, against the fellow who has no money to give them."

"Yes, that's so. I heard that count shouting when he came to our house. 'I can buy you and sell you,' he said."

"And what did the judge say?"

"My father said to him, 'Get out of my house!'"

"There you are! That's what Tiburcy says, that the judge has the courage to throw a man out even if he's rich."

Again and again, I turned this conversation over in my mind. Walek's words had touched a chord of filial pride deep in my heart. It was pleasant to hear my father praised, the more so that the praise came from Tiburcy, who "always knows". But at the same time I ached with an anguished love, mingled with the bitter certainty that my father had never loved me — would never love me — as Tiburcy loved his children.

The grey stone

So the days slipped by until the members of the "bad society" stopped coming to town. Dejectedly, I wandered through the streets on the watch for them, ready at the first sight to hurry up the hill. But they did not come and I grew terribly lonely. It had become a real necessity to me to be with Walek and Marusya. At last one day, as I walked aimlessly along the dusty road, Walek overtook me and laid his hand on my shoulder.

"Why don't you come round any more?" he asked.

"I was afraid to. Your people don't come to town."

"Oh, so that's it! They're all away. You can come if you want to. I thought it was something else."

"What else?"

"I thought you were tired of us."

"No, no! Let's go right away," I cried hastily. "I've even

got some apples with me."

"Look, you go ahead," he said, "and I'll catch up with you on the hill. I've got some things to do in town."

I walked slowly, looking back every now and then for Walek. But I got all the way up the hill, and approached the chapel, and still he had not come into sight. I looked about me. What was I to do? Clearly, I had best wait for Walek. And while I waited, I wandered idly about among the graves, trying to make out the half-obliterated inscriptions on the moss-grown stones.

After a while I came upon a big stone mausoleum, roofless and with crumbling walls. Its door was boarded up. Driven by curiosity, I propped an old cross against the wall, climbed up on it and looked inside. The tomb was empty but there was a window cut into its floor, a real window with glass panes. Through these panes I glimpsed black emptiness.

While I perched there on the wall, wondering at this strange window, Walek came running up the hill, tired and out of breath. He had a loaf of bread in his hand and something bulged under his shirt. His face was streaming with sweat.

"Ho!" he cried, when he saw where I was. "So that's where you are! You won't tell anyone where we live. Come on in."

"In where?" I asked.

"You'll see in a minute. Follow me."

Parting the branches, he ducked in among the bushes along the chapel wall and disappeared. I followed. A few steps brought me out into a bare small space, entirely concealed by vegetation. Between the two bird-cherry tree trunks yawned a large opening in the ground, with earth steps leading down. Walek started down the steps and motioned to me to follow. In a few seconds we were in total darkness underground, and Walek took my hand to guide me. For a while we followed a damp, narrow passageway, then suddenly, after a sharp turn to the right, came into a roomy vault.

I stopped short in the entrance, amazed by the strange sight that met my eyes. The sunlight could not reach these windows directly. It was reflected down to them from the crumbling walls of the tombs. Pouring down through the damp air of the vault, it struck the stone slabs that made the floor and, thrown back from them, cast dull gleams into every corner. The walls, too, were stone. Massive columns, rising heavily from the floor, sent out stone arches to every side. These joined overhead in a vaulted ceiling. Under each of the windows, a human figure sat on the floor. One was the old Professor.

Under the other window sat Marusya, picking over a heap of flowers, as she always liked to do. The light fell on her fair head, on all her tiny figure. Yet, somehow, she hardly stood out at all against the background of grey stone – just an odd, dimly outlined little shadow that seemed on the verge of fading into nothing.

The walls of the vault joined together in heavy arches over the tiny, childish figure. I remembered Walek's talk of the "grey stone" that sucked the life out of Marusya and a superstitious dread crept into my heart. I seemed to feel an invisible, stony stare boring into me as well as Marusya.

"Walek!" Marusya cried joyfully as her brother came in. And when she caught sight of me, her eyes began to sparkle. I gave her my apples and Walek broke his white bread loaf in two and gave half to Marusya and the other half to the Professor.

I felt uncomfortable with the glare of the grey stone upon me.

"Let's get out of here," I said, pulling at Walek's sleeve. "Get her out too."

We went out together into the daylight. Walek seemed more dejected than usual and less inclined to talk.

Tiburcy appears on the scene

I came to the chapel again the following day and we set about showing Marusya how to pull the string of the sparrow-trap we had made for her to play with. Every time an incautious sparrow, attracted by our bait, hopped care-lessly into the trap, she would jerk the string and capture it, then let it go.

Towards noon, however, the sky clouded over. Thunder rolled and then the rain came pouring down. I very much disliked the thought of going underground but, remem-bering that, after all, Walek and Marusya lived there all the time, I conquered my aversion and went inside with them. The vault was dark and very quiet. But we could hear the thunder rolling up above, like a huge cart rumbling over cobblestones.

"Let's play blindman's bluff," I proposed, to cheer us up a

bit. I was the blind man. Marusya toddled about the stone floor on her feeble little legs, bubbling over with her pitiful silvery laughter as I pretended that I could not catch her. Suddenly I bumped into somebody's wet legs and immediately that somebody seized me by the leg and swung me up into the air. The handkerchief fell from my eyes. There was Tiburcy, wet and angry, holding me up by the leg and rolling his eyes in the most frightful way — and all the more frightful that I saw him upside down.

"What is the meaning of this?" he demanded sternly of Walek. "You have good times here, I can see. And pleasant company."

"Let me go!" I screamed, surprised that I could utter a sound at all in such an extraordinary position.

But Tiburcy only grasped my leg the tighter.

"Well?" he demanded, still staring angrily at Walek.

But Walek, in this predicament, found nothing better to do than stuff two fingers into his mouth, as though in proof that there was nothing he could say in reply. I noticed, however, that he was watching me with friendly sympathy as I swung miserably in space like a human pendulum.

Tiburcy lifted me higher, so that he could look into my face.

"Ha! His Honour the judge, if my eyes don't deceive me! And to what do we owe the honour of this visit?"

"Let me go!" I repeated loudly. "Let me go this minute!" Instinctively I tried to stamp my foot — which only made me swing more violently than ever.

Tiburcy laughed aloud.

"Aha! His Honour is pleased to be angry! Well, but you don't know me yet. Tiburcy – that's my name. And I'm going to hang you up over the fire and roast you, just like a little pig."

Walek's frightened eyes seemed to confirm the likelihood of so sad a fate for me. At this point, however, Marusya came to my rescue.

"Don't be scared, Vasya, don't be scared," she said, coming right up to Tiburcy. "He never roasts little boys over the fire. He just made it up."

With a sudden movement, Tiburcy righted me and set me on my feet. I was so dizzy that I almost fell, but he steadied me, and then, sitting down on a block of wood, set me between his knees.

"How did you get in here?" he demanded. "Has this been going on long?"

As I did not answer, he turned to Walek.

"You tell me, then."

"Six days or so."

Tiburcy seemed rather pleased than otherwise by this answer.

"Six whole days!" he exclaimed, turning me round so that he could see my face. "Six days is quite a long time. And you haven't told anyone, in all that time, where you go visiting?"

"No, I haven't."

"Honestly?"

"Honestly."

"Good for you! Then it may be hoped that you won't tell

in the future either. As a matter of fact, I've always thought you a fine boy, seeing you about town. A real tramp, judge or no judge. And will you be judging us some day – eh?"

His tone was quite good-natured now. But I still considered myself insulted and therefore answered sulkily, "I'm no judge, I'm Vasya."

"That makes no difference. Being Vasya is no hindrance to being a judge, and if you're not one now, you may be one later. That's the way the world has always gone. Look at us: I'm Tiburcy, and there is my boy, Walek. I'm a beggar and he's a beggar. I steal at times from hunger and he'll probably steal too. And your father is my judge. Well, and some day you'll be Walek's judge."

"That's not true," I returned sullenly. "I won't ever be a judge over Walek."

"Don't be so sure of that," this odd man said slowly, speaking to me in the tone he might have used to a grown man. Then he continued.

"You don't understand me, of course; you're only a youngster, after all. And so I'll put it to you in this way: if a time ever comes when Walek here is brought up before you to be judged, remember that when the two of you were still young fools and played together – that even then you took your road in whole clothes and with all the food you could eat, and Walek took his in rags and with an empty belly. But for the time being" – his tone changed sharply – "remember this: if you let out a word of what you've seen here to that judge of yours, yes, or to so much as a bird that flies past you in the fields, my name won't be Tiburcy Drab if I don't hang you up by your feet in the fireplace here and make smoked ham of you. That's clear to you, I hope."

"I won't say anything to anybody. I... May I keep coming here?"

"Come if you like, on one condition – what I've already told you about smoked ham. See you don't forget it!"

Evening was gathering when I started down the hill that day, deep in thought, my brain in a pitiful muddle.

Coming through the orchard in the darkness, I bumped suddenly into my father. He was pacing gloomily up and down, as his habit was, with the usual strange, befogged look in his eyes. When I tried to slip past, he laid his hand on my shoulder.

"Where have you been?"

"Just ... walking."

He looked at me intently and seemed about to say something, but then his eyes clouded over again, and with a shrug he strode on down the path.

I had lied to him – for the first time, perhaps, in all my life.

I had always been afraid of my father. Now I feared him all the more, for now I carried within me a whole world of questions and experiences, vague and troublesome. Could he possibly understand me? Could I admit anything to him without treachery to my friends? I trembled at the thought that he might some day learn of my acquaintances, of this "bad society". But I could not betray Walek and Marusya. If I betrayed them and broke my word to them, I could never look them in the eye again for shame.

Autumn

Autumn approached. Harvesting set in and the trees began to yellow. And our Marusya began to ail.

She complained of no aches or pains. But she grew thinner and thinner, paler and paler. Her eyes darkened and seemed bigger than before. It was only by an effort that she could raise her drooping eyelids.

With every visit to the hill I found Marusya worse. She did not go out of doors at all now, and the grey stone – the dark wordless monster of the vaults – pursued its fearful work uninterrupted, sucking the life from her tiny frame. Most of the time she lay in bed and Walek and I did everything we could think of to amuse her, to evoke the faint, silvery music of her laugh.

Now that I was so much in this "bad society", Marusya's smile had grown almost as dear to me as my own sister's. There was no one here to keep reproaching me with my wickedness, no ever-grumbling nurse. Here I was needed. My coming always brought a flush of pleasure to Marusya's cheeks. Walek threw his arms round me like a brother and even Tiburcy, at times, would watch us with a strange look in his eyes and a glint of something that might have been tears.

In the meantime I could feel the gathering of a storm at home. Slipping through the orchard as usual, one morning, I caught sight of my father and with him old Janusz from the castle. The old man was telling my father something, bowing and scraping at every other word. My father listened glumly.

As he listened a sharp furrow of angry impatience cut across his forehead. Then he threw out his arm, as though to brush Janusz from his way.

"Be off with you, old scandalmonger that you are!" he said.

But the old man – blinking strangely, his hat in his hands – only scurried up the path a few steps, and again blocked the way. My father's eyes flashed with anger. Janusz spoke so quietly that I could not make out a word. My father's brusque responses, though, reached me sharp and clear, like the lash of a whip.

"I don't believe a word of it... What have you got against those people? Where is your proof? I won't hear another word."

In the end, my father brushed Janusz aside so decisively that he dared not annoy him further. When Janusz left, my father turned down one of the side paths, and I ran on to the gate.

I had a great dislike for the old owl Janusz, and this encounter made my heart heavy with foreboding. I was certain that the conversation I had overheard concerned my friends – and perhaps myself as well. Tiburcy, when I told him about it, made a terrible face.

"Eh, youngster, but that's unpleasant news. The cursed old hyena!"

The doll

Marusya grew worse. Her great eyes darkened and looked out unmoving, indifferent to all our efforts to amuse her. For many days now we had not heard her laugh. I began bringing her my toys, but even these would occupy her for only the briefest time. I decided to appeal to my sister, Sonya.

Sonya had a big doll with bright pink cheeks and wonderful flaxen hair, the gift of our dead mother. I laid the greatest hopes on that doll. So I called Sonya away from the nurse, down one of the far paths in our orchard, and asked her to give me the doll for a time. At first she only hugged her treasure the tighter. But I begged so earnestly, described to her so vividly the poor, sick child who had never had any toys of her own, that she gave it to me willingly and promised to play with other toys for two or three days and say nothing to anyone about it.

The effect produced by the dainty doll exceeded all my expectations. Marusya, drooping like a flower in the autumn, came suddenly back to life — or so it seemed to me. How she hugged me, and how she laughed and talked with her new playmate! The doll achieved almost a miracle. Confined to her bed for so many days, Marusya got up again and walked about leading her flaxen-haired "daughter" by the hand.

But for me the doll was the cause of many an anxious moment. First of all, there was old Janusz. I passed him in the street when I started for the hill with the doll under my jacket. He looked at me and shook his head. Then, a day or two later, our old nurse noticed that the doll was missing and began to search for it in every corner of the house. My father knew nothing of this as yet. But Janusz came and talked to him again and though he was sent packing with even greater anger than before, my father stopped me on my way to the gate that day and ordered me to stay at home. Next day, too, the order was repeated. It was only four days later, by getting up very early, that I managed to climb the fence and run off before my father woke.

Things were bad on the hill. Marusya was in bed again and worse than ever. Her face was strangely flushed, her fair hair spread in confusion over her pillow. She knew no one at all. Beside her lay the doll, with its rosy cheeks and bright expressionless eyes.

I explained the situation to Walek, and we decided that the doll must be taken home – the more so that Marusya was in no state to notice its disappearance. But we were mistaken. Half conscious as she was, she opened her eyes when I drew the doll away, and stared vacantly before her, as though she did not see me or understand what was going on. Then, suddenly, she began to cry, very softly, but so plaintively and with a look of such poignant grief on her thin face through the mask of delirium that I was frightened and quickly put the doll back in her arms. She smiled and hugged it and I realized that I had been about to deprive my little friend of the last joy of her brief life.

Coming home that day, I again met Janusz. Indoors, I found Sonya with her eyes full of tears, and the old nurse threw me an angry, annihilating glance. She muttered something under her breath with her sunken, withered lips.

My father asked me where I had been. I made my usual answer. He listened gravely, but made no comment. Once more he ordered me firmly not to leave the house without his permission.

A few days later I was summoned to my father in his study. I went in and stopped timidly just inside the door. Through the window opposite, the melancholy autumn sun was looking in. My father was in his armchair, before my mother's portrait. For some time he did not move nor turn his face to me. I could hear the rapid beating of my heart.

At last he turned. I looked up at him, and quickly dropped my eyes. His face was terrifying. Perhaps half a minute passed, during which I could feel his heavy, unmoving, crushing gaze.

"Did you take your sister's doll?"

I started, so sharply, so distinctly did the words descend upon me.

"Yes," I answered, just audibly.

"Didn't you know that it was a gift from Mother, that you ought to treasure her memory? And so – you stole it!"

"No," I said, lifting my head.

"Dare you deny it?" he cried, starting to his feet. "You stole it, and took it away somewhere. Where did you take it? Speak up!"

He strode across the room to me and laid a heavy hand on my shoulder. With an effort, I raised my head and looked up at him. His face was white, his eyes blazing with anger. I shrank from his look.

"Well, then! Speak up!"

His hand weighed still more heavily on my shoulder.

"I ... won't tell," I answered, very low.

"Yes, you will!" he said with strange insistence. Now his voice held a threatening note.

"I won't tell," I whispered, lower still.

"And I say you will! You will!"

His voice faltered, as though he had to force the words out with painful effort. I could feel his hand trembling on my shoulder. I hung my head lower and lower. Tears filled my eyes but still I repeated, barely audibly, "I won't tell. I'll never, never tell you, not for anything."

In those moments, I proved myself my father's son. Not by the most fearful torments could he have got any other answer from me. In response to his threats, my heart swelled with a deep sense of injury – the injury, as yet not clearly understood, of a neglected child – and of poignant love for those who had taken me in so warmly, out there in the ruined chapel.

My father drew a heavy breath. I could feel my body shrinking in his grasp. Bitter tears ran, stinging, down my cheeks. I waited.

He was terribly hot-tempered, I knew. And I knew he was now boiling over with fury. What would he do to me? Even in that dreadful moment I loved my father, and I felt that he was on the verge of some act of wrathful violence that would shatter my love for him beyond repair. I was not afraid any more, not in the least. I stood waiting, as I remember, wishing for an end of it all. If that was how it was to be, why, let it. And all the better. Yes, all the better.

Again my father drew a heavy breath. Perhaps he had conquered his fury. To this day, I do not know. Just at that moment a harsh voice came suddenly in at the open window.

"Ha! My poor young friend!"

Tiburcy! But, though I felt my father's hand on my shoulder quiver at this interruption, it never occurred to me that Tiburcy's coming might stand between my father and myself, might avert that which I considered inevitable.

Tiburcy came quickly into the house and paused in the doorway to the study. His sharp lynx eyes took in the situation immediately.

"Ha! I find my young friend in quite a predicament!"

My father met the intruder with a stare of morose surprise, but Tiburcy did not falter beneath it. He was grave now, and his eyes gazed with an unusual sadness in them.

"Your Honour!" he said quietly. "You are a just man. Let the child go. He's been in bad society, true, but – God's my witness – he's done nothing evil. If he's befriended my poor little ragamuffins, why, I swear to it, you can have me hanged before I'll let him suffer for it. Here's your doll, youngster."

He undid the bundle he was carrying, and there was the doll.

My father's hand relaxed its grip on my shoulder. His face showed his amazement.

"What does all this mean?" he demanded.

"Let the boy go," Tiburcy repeated, and his broad hand gently stroked my bowed head. "You'll get nothing out of him by threats, whereas I'll gladly tell you all you want to know. Shall we go into some other room, Your Honour?"

My father, still staring at Tiburcy amazedly, agreed. They went out of the room together, and I remained alone, overwhelmed by a torrent of emotions that filled my heart to overflowing. At that moment, I knew nothing of what went on around me. There was nothing in the world but a little boy, in whose heart two very differing emotions, wrath and love, had been stirred so violently that everything had clouded over. I was that little boy, and, as I remember it, I was rather sorry for myself. Yes, and there were the voices – two voices, sounding through the shut door in muffled but animated talk.

I was still standing where they had left me when the door opened and they both came in. Again I felt a hand on my head. I started. It was my father's hand, gently stroking my hair.

Tiburcy lifted me and sat me down on his lap – in my father's presence!

"Come to the hill," he said. "Your father will let you come to say goodbye to my little girl. She … she's dead."

Tiburcy's voice shook, and his eyes blinked strangely. But he got up at once, set me down on the floor, threw back his shoulders, and went quickly out of the room.

I looked up questioningly at my father. It was a different man who stood before me now, and in him I sensed the warmth, the kinship, I had so vainly sought before. He stood looking at me in his usual thoughtful way, only now there was a hint of surprise in his eyes, and what seemed to be a question. It was as though the storm that had just passed over us both had swept a dense fog from my father's soul, as though only now had he begun to see me once more as his son.

Taking his hand trustfully, I said, "I didn't steal it, truly. Sonya gave it to me herself, for a few days."

"Yes," he answered slowly, "I know. I've been in the wrong, my boy, and I can only hope that some day you'll try to forget it – won't you?"

Eagerly I seized his hand and kissed it. Never again, I knew now, would he turn on me that dreadful look of a few minutes ago. And love, so long restrained, came flooding hotly into my heart.

I was not afraid of him now.

"May I go to the hill right away?" I asked, recalling Tiburcy's parting words.

"Yes, yes. Go and say goodbye, my boy," he said gently, still with that hint of question in his voice. "Though – wait one minute. Do wait, my boy, just a minute more."

He went out into his bedroom and returned a moment later with some money, which he thrust into my hand.

"Give this to ... Tiburcy. Tell him that I humbly beg him – will you remember? That I humbly beg him – to take this money. In your name. Will you remember? Yes, and tell him ..." – my father seemed to hesitate – "tell him that if he knows a man named Fedorovich, he might warn him that it would be best for him to leave our town. And now go, my boy, go quickly."

Only on the hillside did I catch up with Tiburcy. Clumsily, panting for breath, I did my father's errand.

"Father ... humbly begs..."

And I pressed the money into his hand.

I did not look into his face. He took the money, and received the message concerning Fedorovich in gloomy silence.

Marusya lay on a bench in a dark corner of the vault.

Dead: to a child, the word in itself has not much meaning. It was only now at the sight of that lifeless form that realization came, and I choked with bitter tears. She lay there so grave and sad — my tiny friend, with such a wistful look on her little face. Her eyes were shut. They were a little sunken, and the blue shadows under them were darker than before. Her lips were parted in an expression of childish sadness, as though in response to our sorrow.

The Professor stood beside her, shaking his head apathetically. In a corner of the vault, someone was at work with an axe, making a coffin out of old boards torn from the chapel roof. Others were decking Marusya in autumn flowers. Walek was asleep. In his sleep he quivered nervously. From time to time he drew a deep, sobbing breath.

Soon after the events I have described the members of the "bad society" dispersed.

Tiburcy and Walek disappeared and no one could say where they had gone, just as none could say where they had come from when they appeared in our town.

Sonya and I often visited Marusya's grave. Sometimes too our father would come with us. We liked to sit here on the hill in the shade of a gently whispering birch tree with the town gleaming mistily far below. We read books together here, and thought together, and confided to one another our earliest thoughts and dreams, and hopes and plans of our high-aspiring youth, our hearts overflowing with life and hope.

The Night the Bed Fell

James Thurber

I suppose that the high-water mark of my youth in Columbus, Ohio, was the night the bed fell on my father. It makes a better recitation (unless, as some friends of mine have said, one has heard it five or six times) than it does a piece of writing, for it is almost necessary to throw furniture around, shake doors, and bark like a dog, to lend the proper atmosphere and verisimilitude to what is admittedly a somewhat incredible tale. Still, it did take place.

It happened, then, that my father had decided to sleep in the attic one night, to be away where he could think. My mother opposed the notion strongly because, she said, the old wooden bed up there was unsafe; it was wobbly and the heavy headboard would crash down on father's head in case the bed fell, and kill him. There was no dissuading him, however, and at a quarter past ten he closed the attic door behind him and went up the narrow twisting stairs. We later heard ominous creakings as he crawled into bed. Grandfather, who usually slept in the attic bed when he was with us, had disappeared some days before. (On these occasions he was usually gone six or eight days and returned growling and out of temper, with the news that the federal Union was run by a passel of blockheads and that the Army of the Potomac didn't have any more chance than a fiddler's bitch.)

We had visiting us at this time a nervous first cousin of mine named Briggs Beall, who believed that he was likely to cease breathing when he was asleep. It was his feeling that if he were not awakened every hour during the night, he might die of suffocation. He had been accustomed to setting an alarm clock to ring at intervals until morning, but I persuaded him to abandon this. He slept in my room and I told him that I was such a light sleeper that if anybody quit breathing in the same room with me, I would wake instantly. He tested me the first night – which I had suspected he would – by holding his breath after my regular breathing had convinced him I was asleep. I was not asleep, however, and called to him. This seemed to allay his fears a little, but he took the precaution of putting a glass of spirits of camphor on a little table at the head of his bed. In case I didn't arouse him until he was almost gone, he said, he would sniff the camphor, a powerful reviver. Briggs was not the only member of his family who had his crotchets. Old Aunt Melissa Beall (who could whistle like a man, with two fingers in her mouth) suffered under the premonition that she was destined to die on South High Street, because she had been born on South High Street and married on South High Street. Then there was Aunt Sarah Shoaf, who never went to bed at night without the fear that a burglar was going to get in and blow chloroform under her door through a tube. To avert this calamity – for she was in greater dread of anaesthetics than of losing her household goods – she always piled her money, silverware, and other valuables in a neat stack just outside her bedroom, with a note reading: "This is all I have. Please take it and do not use your chloroform, as this is all I have." Aunt Gracie Shoaf also had a burglar phobia, but she met it with more fortitude. She was confident that burglars had been getting into her house every night for forty years. The fact that she never missed anything was to her no proof to the contrary. She always claimed that she scared them off before they could take anything, by throwing shoes down the hall-way. When she went to bed she piled, where she could get at them handily, all the shoes there were about her house. Five minutes after she had turned off the light, she would sit up in bed and say "Hark!" Her husband, who had learned to ignore the whole situation as long ago as 1903, would either be sound asleep or pretend to be sound asleep. In either case he would not respond to her tugging and pulling, so that presently she would arise, tiptoe to the door, open it slightly and heave a shoe down the hall in one direction, and its mate down the hall in the other direction. Some nights she threw them all, some nights only a couple of pair.

But I am straying from the remarkable incidents that took place during the night that the bed fell on father. By mid-night we were all in bed. The layout of the rooms and the disposition of their occupants is important to an under-standing of what later occurred. In the front room upstairs (just under father's attic bedroom) were my mother and my brother Herman, who sometimes sang in his sleep, usually "Marching Through Georgia" or "Onward, Christian Sol-diers". Briggs Beall and myself were in a room adjoining this one. My brother Roy was in a room across the hall from ours. Our bull terrier, Rex, slept in the hall.

My bed was an army cot, one of those affairs which are made wide enough to sleep on comfortably only by putting up, flat with the middle section, the two sides which ordinarily hang down like the sideboards of a drop-leaf table. When these sides are up, it is perilous to roll too far toward the edge, for then the cot is likely to tip completely over, bringing the whole bed down on top of one, with a tremendous banging crash. This, in fact, is precisely what happened, about two o'clock in the morning. (It was my mother who, in recalling the scene later, first referred to it as "the night the bed fell on your father".)

Always a deep sleeper, slow to arouse (I had lied to Briggs), I was at first unconscious of what had happened when the iron cot rolled me on to the floor and toppled over on me. It left me still warmly bundled up and unhurt, for the bed rested above me like a canopy. Hence I did not wake up, only reached the edge of consciousness and went back. The racket, however, instantly awakened my mother, in the next room, who came to the immediate conclusion that her worst dread was realized: the big wooden bed upstairs had fallen on father. She therefore screamed, "Let's go to your poor father!" It was this shout, rather than the noise of my cot falling, that awakened Herman, in the same room with her. He thought that mother had become, for no apparent reason, hysterical. "You're all right, Mamma!" he shouted, trying to calm her. They exchanged shout for shout for perhaps ten seconds: "Let's go to your poor father!" and "You're all right!" That woke up Briggs. By this time I was conscious of what was going on, in a vague way, but did not yet realize that I was under my bed instead of on it. Briggs, awakening in the midst of loud shouts of fear and apprehension, came to the quick conclusion that he was suffocating and that we were all trying to "bring him out". With a low moan, he grasped the glass of camphor at the head of his bed and instead of sniffing it poured it over himself. The room reeked of camphor. "Ugf, ahfg," choked Briggs, like a drowning man, for he had almost succeeded in stopping his breath under the deluge of pungent spirits. He leaped out of bed and groped toward the open window, but he came up against one that was closed. With his hand, he beat out the glass, and I could hear it crash and tinkle on the alleyway below. It was at this juncture that I, in trying to get up, had the uncanny sensation of feeling my bed above me! Foggy with sleep, I now suspected, in my turn, that the whole uproar was being made in a frantic endeavour to extricate me from what must be an unheard-of and perilous situation. "Get me out of this!" I bawled. "Get me out!" I think I had the nightmarish belief that I was entombed in a mine. "Gugh," gasped Briggs, floundering in his camphor.

By this time my mother, still shouting, pursued by Herman, still shouting, was trying to open the door to the attic, in order to go up and get my father's body out of the wreckage. The door was stuck, however, and wouldn't yield. Her frantic pulls on it only added to the general banging and confusion. Roy and the dog were up, the one shouting questions, the other barking.

142

Father, farthest away and soundest sleeper of all, had by this time awakened by the battering on the attic door. He decided that the house was on fire. "I'm coming, I'm coming!" he wailed in a slow, sleepy voice – it took him many minutes to regain full consciousness. My mother, still believing he was caught under the bed, detected in his "I'm coming!" the mournful, resigned note of one who is preparing to meet his Maker. "He's dying!" she shouted.

"I'm all right!" Briggs yelled to reassure her. "I'm all right!" He still believed that it was his own closeness to death that was worrying mother. I found at last the light switch in my room, unlocked the door, and Briggs and I joined the others at the attic door. The dog, who never did like Briggs, jumped for him – assuming that he was the culprit in whatever was going on – and Roy had to throw Rex and hold him. We could hear father crawling out of bed upstairs. Roy pulled the attic door open, with a mighty jerk, and father came down the stairs, sleepy and irritable but safe and sound. My mother began to weep when she saw him. Rex began to howl. "What in the name of God is going on here?" asked father.

The situation was finally put together like a gigantic jig-saw puzzle. Father caught a cold from prowling around in his bare feet but there were no other bad results. "I'm glad," said mother, who always looked on the bright side of things, "that your grandfather wasn't here."

Roosya

Ivan Bunin

At eleven o'clock at night the fast train from Moscow to
Sevastopol stopped at a little station beyond Podolsk, where
it was not scheduled to stop, and waited for something on
the other line. In the train a gentleman and a lady came up
to the lowered window of a first-class carriage. A conductor
walked across the railway track with a red lamp swinging
from his arm, and the lady asked:

"Tell me, why are we waiting here?"

The conductor answered that the post train was late.

It was dark and gloomy in the station. Twilight had fallen
long ago, but beyond the platform in the west the prolonged
sunset glow of a Moscow summer still cast a dying light
over the blackening wooded plains. A damp marshy smell
entered through the open window. In the stillness one could
hear from somewhere the monotonous croaking of a corn-
crake, a sound evoking, somehow, yet another sensation of
dampness.

He stood with his elbow against the window-frame; she
leaned on his shoulder.

"I lived once in this neighbourhood during my holidays,"
he said. "I was doing a tutoring job in one of the villas,
five versts away from here. A boring place. Patchy little

pinewoods, magpies, mosquitoes and crickets... There was no proper view from anywhere. One could only admire the horizon from the upper floor of the villa. The house was built of course in the Russian villa style and was sadly neglected — the owners had become impoverished — behind the house something like a garden grew, and beyond that garden stretched a cross between a lake and a swamp, overgrown with rushes and yellow water-lilies, and with the inevitable flat-bottomed boat moored alongside the muddy bank."

"And, of course, a bored young lady on holiday, whom you took boating on that swamp."

"Yes, just as you suppose. Only the young lady was not at all bored. I went boating with her chiefly at night, and the whole affair took a quiet poetic turn. The sky in the west kept all night a greenish transparent tint, and like now, over there on the horizon, it went on glowing and glowing... Only a single oar was available and that was more like a spade — I pulled at it like a savage, plunging it from one side to another. The opposite bank was darkened by low woods, but above it glowed that strange perpetual twilight. And everywhere an inconceivable stillness — broken only by the buzzing of mosquitoes and the whirr of dragonflies in flight. I never thought that they flew about at night — it seemed they had some reason for flying — that was quite frightening."

At last the thunder of an approaching train made itself heard, it came nearer and rushed by with a windy roar, fused into one luminous yellow strip of lit-up windows. Our train at once started to move. The attendant came into the carriage, switched on the light and set about preparing the bunks for the night.

"Well, and what happened to you and that young lady? Was it a real love-story? Why did you never tell me about her before? What did she look like?"

"Tall and thin. She wore a yellow cotton sarafan and on her bare legs peasant shoes plaited out of various bright-coloured wools."

"So that was also in Russian style."

"I think it was more in the style of poverty. Having nothing else to wear, she fell back on the sarafan. Besides, she was an artist, she studied painting in the Stroganov Institute. She was herself picturesque, like an ikon-painting. A large dark pigtail hung down her back, her face was swarthy with dark little moles, a straight regular nose, black eyes, black eyebrows... Her hair was dry and thick, slightly curling. All that with the yellow sarafan and broad white muslin sleeves combined to create a most charming effect. Her ankles and feet in their loose shoes were austere, the bones protruding from under her delicate brown skin."

"I know that type. I had a friend like that at school. Probably she was hysterical."

"Maybe. All the more so since facially she was like her mother, some kind of princess with eastern blood, who suffered from a brooding melancholia. She only appeared at meal times. She came in, sat down in silence, and coughed, without raising her eyes, shifting her knife and fork from side to side. If she suddenly said something, it was so unexpected and loud that one jumped."

"And the father?"

146

"Also silent and dry, a tall man, a retired officer. Only their son was a straightforward attractive boy. I was tutoring him."

The attendant came out of the coupé, said that the beds were ready and wished them a good night.

"What was her name?"

"Roosya."

"What kind of a name is that?"

"Very simple – short for Maroosya."

"Well, so you were very much in love with her?"

"Of course I seemed to be, quite dreadfully."

"And she?"

He paused and answered drily.

"Probably it seemed the same to her. But let us go to bed. I'm terribly tired after today."

"I like that! So my interest was in vain. Come, tell me in two words how your love-story ended."

"In nothing. I went away, and that was the end."

"Why didn't you marry her?"

"Obviously I had a premonition I would meet you."

"No, seriously?"

"Well, because I shot myself and she stabbed herself with a dagger..."

They washed their faces, cleaned their teeth, shut themselves up in the stuffy interior of the coupé, undressed and lay down with relief under the fresh glossy linen sheets, their heads resting on the white pillows which slipped down from the raised tops of the beds.

The blue-mauve aperture over the door looked like an

eye into the darkness. She soon went to sleep, he lay awake, smoked and returned in his thoughts to that summer...

On her body too there were many little dark moles – it was a delightful peculiarity. Because she walked in soft shoes, without heels, her whole body moved under the yellow sarafan. It was a wide thin sarafan, which gave full freedom to her long virgin body. One day she got her feet wet in the rain, and ran from the garden into the drawing-room; he dashed in to help her pull off her shoes and kissed her wet narrow feet – he had never known such happiness in his life. The fresh fragrant rain poured down ever faster and heavier, clattering on the balcony beyond the open doors; in the darkened house everyone was sleeping after lunch – and how he was frightened out of his wits when a cock, its black feathers shot with iridescent green and with a huge red comb, suddenly also ran in from the garden, its claws tapping across the floor, just at that intimate moment when they had forgotten all precaution. Seeing how they jumped up from the sofa, the cock hurriedly turned back, lowering his head as if from a sense of delicacy, and ran out again into the rain with his shining tail bedraggled...

At first she kept on looking at him; when he said something to her, she blushed deeply and answered in a soft bantering tone; at table she often teased him, turning to her father with loud remarks: "Don't offer him anything, Father, it's useless. He doesn't like cheese dumplings. He doesn't like cold kvass soup or noodles, he despises sour milk and hates milk cheese."

In the mornings he was busy teaching the boy, and she

with household jobs – she had to look after everything in the house. They had lunch at one, and after lunch she went to her room upstairs, or, if the weather was fine, into the garden, where her easel stood under a birch-tree; whisking away the mosquitoes, she painted landscapes there. Then she would come on to the balcony where he sat after lunch reading a book in a sloping wicker armchair; she would stand, clasping her hands behind her back, and looking at him with an uncertain smile.

"May I ask what wisdom you are deigning to study?"

"The history of the French Revolution."

"Oh, my God! I had no idea that we are sheltering a revolutionary in the house."

"But why have you abandoned your painting?"

"Oh, I shall give it up completely. I am convinced now that I have no talent."

"But show me a few of your sketches."

"But do you imagine that you know anything about painting?"

"You are very ambitious."

"That is my fault..."

One day she suggested he should take her rowing on the lake, and suddenly said in a decisive tone of voice:

"Our tropical rainy season seems to have come to an end. Let us go out and enjoy ourselves. Of course our boat is a bit rotten and has several holes in the bottom, but Petya and I have stopped up all the holes with water-weeds..."

It was a hot steamy day. Along the bank the tall grass, speckled with tiny yellow flowers, breathed out a languid sultry warmth and over it flitted and hovered innumerable greenish white butterflies.

Adapting himself to her constantly bantering tone, he went up to the boat and remarked:

"At last you have deigned to descend to my level!"

"At last you have summoned up courage to answer me!" — she promptly retorted and jumped into the prow of the boat, frightening the frogs who splashed into the water from all sides — but suddenly she screamed shrilly, and pulled her sarafan right up to her knees, stamping her feet:

"A snake! A grass-snake!"

He caught a fleeting glimpse of her darkly shining naked legs, seized the oar from the prow, beat down the snake wriggling on the bottom of the boat, crushed it and threw it far off into the water.

She was pale with a kind of Indian pallor, the moles on her face had darkened, her black hair and eyes had turned even darker. She heaved a sigh of relief:

"Oh, how nauseating! Obviously the word horror (oojas) comes from grass-snake (ooj). They are all round us here, in the garden and under the house... And Petya, just think of it, picks them up in his hands!"

For the first time she was speaking frankly to him, and for the first time they looked each other straight in the eyes.

"You're a fine fellow — how you knocked that snake out properly!"

She became quite expansive, smiled, ran from the prow into the stern and sat down gaily. In her fright what struck him was her beauty, and he thought tenderly: "Yes, she is still completely a young girl!" But, putting on an indifferent preoccupied look, he got into the boat, and leaning with his oar on the damp bottom he wheeled it round and pulled it through the tangled thicket of water-weeds among the green clumps of rushes and the flowering water-lilies, which covered everything in front with their thick luxuriant round foliage. He steered the boat into the open water, and sat down on the centre seat, dipping his oar from side to side like in a canoe.

"Isn't this grand?" she exclaimed.

"Certainly!" he answered, removing his cap, and turned towards her. "Please keep this near you, otherwise I shall knock it into that trough, which, excuse me, is still leaking and full of leeches."

She put the cap on her knees.

"But don't worry, throw it down anywhere."

She pressed the cap to her breast.

"No, I shall keep guard over it!"

Once again his heart throbbed tenderly, but again he turned away and began to paddle with vigorous strokes through the water which glistened among the green and yellow vegetation. Midges began to settle on his face and hands, the warm silver light all round was almost blinding; the steamy air, the shifting rays of sunlight, the curly whiteness of the clouds shining softly in the sky, cast reflections in the water between islands of weed and lilies; everywhere the water was so shallow that one could see the bottom with its carpet of green vegetation, but that in no way interfered with the impression of bottomless depth engulfing the

reflections of sky and clouds. Suddenly she screamed again
– and the boat turned over on its side; she had thrust her
hand over the stern into the water, and seizing the stem of a
water-lily, had pulled it so violently towards her that she fell
over on one side together with the boat – he just managed
to jump forward in time to pull her back by her armpits. She
burst out laughing, and falling down with her back along the
stern she splashed him straight in the face with her wet hand.
Then he caught hold of her again, and without knowing
what he was doing, he kissed her laughing lips. She quickly
threw her arms round his neck and kissed him clumsily on
the cheek...

From that time they started going out in the boat at night.
The next day she summoned him into the garden after lunch
and asked:

"Do you love me?"

He answered warmly, remembering yesterday's kisses in
the boat:

"From the very first day we met!"

"And I—" she said. "No, at first I hated you – it seemed
you never noticed me at all. But, thank God, all that is over.
This evening, after they have all gone to bed, go to the same
place again and wait for me. Only leave the house as cautiously as you can – Mama watches every step I take, she's
madly jealous."

That night she came to the shore carrying a rug over her
arm. He met her with embarrassed joy, and only asked:

"Why have you brought a rug?"

"How stupid you are! We shall be cold. Well, climb in

quickly and row to the opposite bank…"

They remained silent all the time. When they had reached the wood on the other side she said to him: "Well, here we are. Now come to me. Where is the rug? Ah, it's at my feet. Cover me, I'm shivering, and sit down. Like this… No, wait a moment, yesterday we kissed each other accidentally somehow, now I will kiss you first, only softly, softly. And you embrace me … everywhere…"

She was only wearing a nightdress under her sarafan. Tenderly, scarcely touching, she kissed him on the edge of the lips. He, with his mind in a whirl, pushed her against the stern. She embraced him in an ecstasy…

For a time she lay exhausted, then she raised herself, and with a smile of tired happiness and still lingering pain she said:

"Now we are husband and wife. Mama says she will never survive my marriage, but I don't want to think of that now… Do you know, I want to bathe, how I love it at night…"

She drew her clothes off over her head, her whole body glowing in the half-light, and began to arrange her pigtail round her head, raising her arms, showing her dark armpits and rising breasts, unashamed of her nakedness and the dark patch under her belly. Having fastened her hair she jumped up, kissed him quickly, and plunged into the water with a splash; she threw back her head and kicked up the water noisily.

Afterwards he hurriedly helped her to dress and wrapped her in the rug. Her black eyes and black plaited hair looked fantastic in the dusk. He no longer dared to touch her, he only kissed her hands and could not speak for unbearable happiness. All the time it seemed that someone was there in the dark woods along the shore, where now and then a glow-worm twinkled silently – someone was standing there and listening. From time to time something rustled mysteriously. She raised her head:

"Stop, what was that?"

"Don't be afraid, it's probably a frog climbing up the bank. Or a hedgehog in the wood…"

"But what if it's a goat?"

"What kind of goat?"

"I don't know. But just think; a goat comes out of the wood, stands and watches us… I feel so wonderful, I want to talk the most arrant nonsense!"

Again he pressed her hands to his lips, and kissed her cold breast like something sacred. How she had become for him a completely new being! And the greenish half-light still glowed unchanged over the low dark woods, faintly reflected in the water whitening the flat distance; a pungent smell like celery rose from the plants along the bank; invisible mosquitoes hummed strangely, querulously – and the uncanny sleepless dragonflies flew and flew, passing with a gentle whirr over the boat and on over the night-lit water. And all the time somewhere something rustled, crawled, stole its way through…

A week later he was turned out of the house in an ugly shameful manner, quite shattered by the horror of such a sudden and abrupt parting.

They were sitting after lunch in the drawing-room, their

heads close together, looking through pictures in an old number of *Niva*.

"You haven't grown tired of me yet?" he asked quietly, pretending to look attentively at the pictures.

"Stupid. Terribly stupid!" she whispered.

Suddenly they heard soft running steps — and on the threshold in a torn black silk dressing-gown and worn-out Morocco slippers appeared her half-mad mother. Her black eyes flashed tragically. She ran forward, as if she were on the stage, and cried out:

"I understood everything! I felt it, I kept watch! You scoundrel, she will never be yours!"

And raising her arm in her long sleeve, she fired with a deafening report an ancient pistol, which Petya used to frighten away sparrows, loading it only with powder. He rushed at her through the smoke, and seized her clenched hand. She tore herself away, knocked him on the forehead with the pistol, cutting his brow which started to bleed; her cries and the pistol shot had roused the people in the house; hearing their footsteps she flung the pistol at him and began to shout even more theatrically, foaming at the mouth:

"Over my dead body only will she come to you! If she runs away with you, I shall hang myself that very day, I'll throw myself from the roof! Get out of my house, you scoundrel! Marya Victorovna, choose between us — your mother or him!"

"You, you, mother..." she whispered distractedly...

He woke up, opened his eyes — through the black darkness the blue-mauve aperture over the door still watched him

155

like an eye, inexorable, enigmatic – and the carriage, swaying on its springs, rushed onward at the same steady speed.
Already they had left that sad little station miles and miles
behind them. And all this had happened a whole twenty
years ago – woods, magpies, marsh, water-lilies, snakes and
storks – yes, there were storks as well – how they had all
slipped out of his memory! Everything was extraordinary in
that amazing summer; it was extraordinary how a pair of
those storks flew at intervals to the edge of the marsh, how
they allowed nobody but her to come near them, and, bending their long thin necks, scrutinized her from above with a
very grave but benevolent curiosity, while she, running up to
them with soft light steps in her plaited shoes, suddenly sat
down on her heels, holding up her yellow sarafan over the
moist warm plants on the bank, and with childish eagerness
looked into the beautiful severe black pupils of their eyes,
tightly encircled by dark grey rings. He watched her and
them from far – through a pair of field-glasses, and saw distinctly their small glossy heads – their bony nostrils, the
chinks in their huge powerful beaks, with one blow of which
they could kill a snake. Their stumpy bodies and the fluffy
down on their tails were tightly covered with steel-covered
plumage, their scaly legs like canes were quite dispropor-
tionately long and thin – black on one of them, greenish on
another. Sometimes they both stood for whole hours on one
leg, inexplicably motionless, at other times they jumped
about for no apparent reason, and spread out their enormous
wings; occasionally they walked about with a pompous
important air, raising their feet in slow regular steps,

pressing three of their toes into a ball, then stretching them out like the claws of a bird of prey, and all the time they kept on nodding their heads… Of course when she ran up to them, he could think of nothing but her and saw nothing else – he could only see her raised sarafan, and a piercing languid tremor ran through him at the thought of the brown body under it, and of her little dark moles. But on that last day, that last time they were sitting together on the sofa, looking through the bound volume of old *Nivas*, she was also holding his cap in her hands, clasping it to her breast, as she had done in the boat, and she said, looking at him with a happy twinkle in her black mirror-like eyes:

"But now I love you so much that nothing is dearer to me than even that smell from inside your cap, that smell of your head and your nasty eau-de-Cologne!"

* * *

When the train had passed Kursk, they were sitting in the restaurant-car, and he drank brandy with his coffee; his wife said to him:

"Why are you drinking so much? I think that's already your fifth glass. Are you still pining for the memory of your holiday girl with the bony feet?"

"Indeed, I am pining," he answered, with a short unpleasant laugh. "The holiday girl… *Amata nobis quantum amabitur nulla!*"*

"Is that Latin? What does it mean?"

"You don't need to know that."

"How bad your manners are," she said, heaved a careless sigh, and began to look out of the sunlit window.

* "Beloved by me as no woman will ever be loved again" Catullus, Poem VIII.

The Tell-Tale Heart

Edgar Allan Poe

True! — nervous — very, very dreadfully nervous I had been and am; but why *will* you say that I am mad? The disease had sharpened my senses — not destroyed — not dulled them. Above all was the sense of hearing acute. I heard all things in the heaven and in the earth. I heard many things in hell. How, then, am I mad? Hearken! and observe how healthily — how calmly I can tell you the whole story.

It is impossible to say how first the idea entered my brain; but once conceived, it haunted me day and night. Object there was none. Passion there was none. I loved the old man. He had never wronged me. He had never given me insult. For his gold I had no desire. I think it was his eye! yes, it was this! One of his eyes resembled that of a vulture — a pale blue eye, with a film over it. Whenever it fell upon me, my blood ran cold; and so by degrees — very gradually — I made up my mind to take the life of the old man, and thus rid myself of the eye for ever.

Now this is the point. You fancy me mad. Madmen know nothing. But you should have seen *me*. You should have seen how wisely I proceeded — with what caution — with what foresight — with what dissimulation I went to work! I was never kinder to the old man than during the whole week before I killed him. And every night, about midnight, I turned the latch of his door and opened it – oh so gently! And then, when I had made an opening sufficient for my head, I put in a dark lantern, all closed, closed, so that no light shone out, and then I thrust in my head. Oh, you would have laughed to see how cunningly I thrust it in! I moved it slowly – very, very slowly, so that I might not disturb the old man's sleep. It took me an hour to place my whole head within the opening so far that I could see him as he lay upon his bed. Ha! – would a madman have been so wise as this? And then, when my head was well in the room, I undid the lantern, cautiously – oh, so cautiously – cautiously (for the hinges creaked) I undid it just so much that a single thin ray fell upon the vulture eye. And this I did for seven long nights – every night just at midnight – but I found the eye always closed; and so it was impossible to do the work; for it was not the old man who vexed me, but his Evil Eye. And every morning, when the day broke, I went boldly into the chamber, and spoke courageously to him, calling him by name in a hearty tone, and inquiring how he had passed the night. So you see he would have been a very profound old man, indeed, to suspect that every night, just at twelve, I looked in upon him while he slept.

Upon the eighth night I was more than usually cautious in opening the door. A watch's minute hand moves more quickly than did mine. Never before that night had I *felt* the extent of my own powers – of my sagacity. I could scarcely contain my feelings of triumph. To think that there I was, opening the door, little by little, and he not even to dream of my secret deeds or thoughts. I fairly chuckled at the idea; and perhaps he heard me – for he moved on the bed suddenly, as if startled. Now you may think that I drew back – but no. His room was as black as pitch with the thick darkness (for the shutters were close fastened, through fear of robbers), and so I knew that he could not see the opening of the door, and I kept pushing it on steadily, steadily.

I had my head in, and was about to open the lantern, when my thumb slipped upon the tin fastening, and the old man sprang up in the bed, crying out, "Who's there?"

I kept quite still and said nothing. For a whole hour I did not move a muscle, and in the meantime I did not hear him lie down. He was still sitting up in the bed, listening – just as I have done, night after night, hearkening to the deathwatches in the wall.

Presently I heard a slight groan, and I knew it was the groan of mortal terror. It was not a groan of pain or of grief – oh, no! – it was the low stifled sound that arises from the bottom of the soul when overcharged with awe. I knew the sound well. Many a night, just at midnight, when all the world slept, it has welled up from my own bosom, deepening, with its dreadful echo, the terrors that distracted me. I say I knew it well. I knew what the old man felt, and pitied him, although I chuckled at heart. I knew that he had been lying awake ever since the first slight noise, when he had turned in the bed. His fears had been ever since growing upon him. He had been trying to fancy them causeless, but could not. He had been saying to himself, "It is nothing but the wind in the chimney – it is only a mouse crossing the floor," or, "It is merely a cricket which has made a single chirp." Yes, he had been trying to comfort himself with these suppositions; but he had found all in vain. *All in vain,* because Death, in approaching him, had stalked with his black shadow before him, and enveloped the victim. And it was the mournful influence of the unperceived shadow that caused him to feel – although he neither saw nor heard – to *feel* the presence of my head within the room.

When I had waited a long time, very patiently, without hearing him lie down, I resolved to open a little – a very, very little crevice in the lantern. So I opened it – you cannot imagine how stealthily, stealthily – until, at length, a single dim ray, like the thread of the spider, shot from out the crevice and fell upon the vulture eye.

It was open – wide, wide open – and I grew furious as I gazed upon it. I saw it with perfect distinctness – all a dull blue, with a hideous veil over it that chilled the very marrow in my bones; but I could see nothing else of the old man's face or person, for I had directed the ray, as if by instinct, precisely upon the damned spot.

And have I not told you that what you mistake for madness is but over acuteness of the senses? – now, I say, there came to my ears a low, dull, quick sound, such as a watch makes when enveloped in cotton. I knew *that* sound well, too. It was the beating of the old man's heart. It increased my fury, as the beating of a drum stimulates the soldier into courage.

But even yet I refrained and kept still. I scarcely breathed. I held the lantern motionless. I tried how steadily I could maintain the ray upon the eye. Meantime the hellish tattoo of the heart increased. It grew quicker and quicker, and louder and louder every instant. The old man's terror *must* have been extreme! It grew louder, I say, louder every moment! – do you mark me well? I have told you that I am nervous: so I am. And now, at the dead hour of the night, amid the dreadful silence of that old house, so strange a noise as this excited me to uncontrollable terror. Yet, for some minutes longer, I refrained and stood still. But the beating grew louder, louder! I thought the heart must burst. And now a new anxiety seized me – the sound would be heard by a neighbour! The old man's hour had come! With a loud yell I threw open the lantern and leaped into the room. He shrieked once – once only. In an instant I dragged him to the floor, and pulled the heavy bed over him. I then smiled gaily, to find the deed so far done. But, for many minutes, the heart beat on with a muffled sound. This, however, did not vex me; it would not be heard through the wall. At length it ceased. The old man was dead. I removed the bed and examined the corpse. Yes, he was stone, stone dead. I placed my hand upon the heart and held it there many minutes. There was no pulsation. He was stone dead. His eye would trouble me no more.

If still you think me mad, you will think so no longer when I describe the wise precautions I took for the concealment of the body. The night waned, and I worked hastily, but in silence. First of all I dismembered the corpse. I cut off the head and the arms and the legs.

I then took up three planks from the flooring of the chamber, and deposited all between the scantlings. I then replaced the boards so cleverly, so cunningly, that no human eye – not even *his* – could have detected anything wrong. There was nothing to wash out – no stain of any kind – no blood-spot whatever. I had been too wary for that. A tub had caught all – ha! ha!

When I had made an end of these labors, it was four o'clock – still dark as midnight. As the bell sounded the hour, there came a knocking at the street door. I went down to open it with a light heart – for what had I *now* to fear? There entered three men, who introduced themselves, with perfect suavity, as officers of the police. A shriek had been heard by a neighbour during the night; suspicion of foul play had been aroused; information had been lodged at the police office, and they (the officers) had been deputed to search the premises.

I smiled – for *what* had I to fear? I bade the gentlemen welcome. The shriek, I said, was my own in a dream. The old man, I mentioned, was absent in the country. I took my visitors all over the house. I bade them search – search *well*. I led them, at length, to *his* chamber. I showed them his treasures, secure, undisturbed. In the enthusiasm of my confidence, I brought chairs into the room, and desired them *here* to rest from their fatigues, while I myself, in the wild audacity of my perfect triumph, placed my own seat upon the very spot beneath which reposed the corpse of the victim.

The officers were satisfied. My *manner* had convinced them. I was singularly at ease. They sat, and while I answered cheerily, they chatted of familiar things. But, ere long, I felt myself getting pale and wished them gone. My head ached, and I fancied a ringing in my ears; but still they sat and still chatted. The ringing became more distinct – it continued and became more distinct. I talked more freely to get rid of the feeling; but it continued and gained definitiveness – until, at length, I found that the noise was *not* within my ears.

No doubt I now grew *very* pale; but I talked more fluently, and with a heightened voice. Yet the sound increased – and what could I do? It was *a low, dull, quick sound – much such a sound as a watch makes when enveloped in cotton.* I gasped for breath – and yet the officers heard it not. I talked more quickly – more vehemently; but the noise steadily increased. I arose and argued about trifles, in a high key and with violent gesticulations; but the noise steadily increased. Why *would* they not be gone? I paced the floor to and fro with heavy strides, as if excited to fury by the observations of the men – but the noise steadily increased. O God! what *could* I do? I foamed – I raved – I swore! I swung the chair upon which I had been sitting, and grated it upon the boards, but the noise arose over all and continually increased. It grew louder – louder – *louder!* And still the men chatted pleasantly, and smiled. Was it possible they heard not? Almighty God! – no, no! They heard! – they suspected! – they *knew!* – they were making a mockery of my horror! – this I thought, and this I think. But anything was better than this agony! Anything was more tolerable than this derision! I could bear those hypocritical smiles no longer! I felt that I must scream or die! – and now – again! – hark! louder! louder! louder! *louder!*

"Villains!" I shrieked, "dissemble no more! I admit the deed! – tear up the planks! – here, here! – it is the beating of his hideous heart!"

Borrowing a Match

Stephen Leacock

You might think that borrowing a match upon the street is a simple thing. But any man who has ever tried it will assure you that it is not, and will be prepared to swear to the truth of my experience of the other evening.

I was standing on the corner of the street with a cigar that I wanted to light. I had no match. I waited till a decent, ordinary-looking man came along. Then I said:

"Excuse me, sir, but could you oblige me with the loan of a match?"

"A match?" he said, "why certainly." Then he unbuttoned his overcoat and put his hand in the pocket of his waistcoat. "I know I have one," he went on, "and I'd almost swear it's in the bottom pocket – or, hold on, though, I guess it may be in the top – just wait till I put these parcels down on the sidewalk."

"Oh, don't trouble," I said, "it's really of no consequence."

"Oh, it's no trouble, I'll have it in a minute; I know there must be one in here somewhere" – he was digging his fingers into his pockets as he spoke – "but you see this isn't the waistcoat I generally…"

I saw that the man was getting excited about it. "Well, never mind," I protested; "if that isn't the waistcoat that you generally – why, it doesn't matter."

"Hold on, now, hold on!" the man said, "I've got one of the cursed things in here somewhere. I guess it must be in with my watch. No, it's not there either. Wait till I try my coat. If that confounded tailor only knew enough to make a pocket so that a man could get at it!"

He was getting pretty well worked up now. He had thrown down his walking-stick and was plunging at his pockets with his teeth set. "It's that cursed young boy of mine," he hissed; "this comes of his fooling in my pockets. By Gad! perhaps I won't warm him up when I get home. Say, I'll bet that it's in my hip-pocket. You just hold up the tail of my overcoat a second till I…"

"No, no," I protested again, "please don't take all this trouble, it really doesn't matter. I'm sure you needn't take off your overcoat, and oh, pray don't throw away your letters and things in the snow like that, and tear out your pockets by the roots! Please, please don't trample over your overcoat and put your feet through the parcels. I do hate to hear you swearing at your little boy, with that peculiar whine in your voice. Don't – please don't tear your clothes so savagely."

Suddenly the man gave a grunt of exultation, and drew his hand up from inside the lining of his coat.

"I've got it," he cried. "Here you are!" Then he brought it out under the light.

It was a toothpick.

Yielding to the impulse of the moment I pushed him under the wheels of a trolley-car, and ran.

Lamb to the Slaughter

Roald Dahl

The room was warm and clean, the curtains drawn, the two table lamps alight – hers and the one by the empty chair opposite. On the sideboard behind her, two tall glasses, soda water, whisky. Fresh ice cubes in the Thermos bucket.

Mary Maloney was waiting for her husband to come home from work.

Now and again she would glance up at the clock, but without anxiety, merely to please herself with the thought that each minute gone by made it nearer the time when he would come. There was a slow smiling air about her, and about everything she did. The drop of the head as she bent over her sewing was curiously tranquil. Her skin – for this was her sixth month with child – had acquired a wonderful translucent quality, the mouth was soft, and the eyes, with their new placid look, seemed larger, darker than before.

When the clock said ten minutes to five, she began to listen, and a few moments later, punctually as always, she heard the tyres on the gravel outside, and the car door slamming, the footsteps passing the window, the key turning in the lock. She laid aside her sewing, stood up, and went forward to kiss him as he came in.

"Hullo, darling," she said.

"Hullo," he answered.

She took his coat and hung it in the closet. Then she walked over and made the drinks, a strongish one for him, a weak one for herself; and soon she was back again in her chair with the sewing, and he in the other, opposite, holding the tall glass with both his hands, rocking it so the ice cubes tinkled against the side.

For her, this was always a blissful time of day. She knew he didn't want to speak much until the first drink was finished, and she, on her side, was content to sit quietly, enjoying his company after the long hours alone in the house. She loved to luxuriate in the presence of this man, and to feel — almost as a sunbather feels the sun — that warm male glow that came out of him to her when they were alone together. She loved him for the way he sat loosely in a chair, for the way he came in a door, or moved slowly across the room with long strides. She loved the intent, far look in his eyes when they rested on her, the funny shape of the mouth, and especially the way he remained silent about his tiredness, sitting still with himself until the whisky had taken some of it away.

"Tired, darling?"

"Yes," he said. "I'm tired." And as he spoke, he did an unusual thing. He lifted his glass and drained it in one swallow although there was still half of it, at least half of it, left. She wasn't really watching him but she knew what he had done because she heard the ice cubes falling back against the bottom of the empty glass when he lowered his arm. He paused a moment, leaning forward in the chair, then he got up and went slowly over to fetch himself another.

"I'll get it!" she cried, jumping up.

"Sit down," he said.

When he came back, she noticed that the new drink was dark amber with the quantity of whisky in it.

"Darling, shall I get your slippers?"

"No."

She watched him as he began to sip the dark yellow drink, and she could see little oily swirls in the liquid because it was so strong.

"I think it's a shame," she said, "that when a policeman gets to be as senior as you, they keep him walking about on his feet all day long."

He didn't answer, so she bent her head again and went on with her sewing; but each time he lifted the drink to his lips, she heard the ice cubes clinking against the side of the glass.

"Darling," she said. "Would you like me to get you some cheese? I haven't made any supper because it's Thursday."

"No," he said.

"If you're too tired to eat out," she went on, "it's still not too late. There's plenty of meat and stuff in the freezer, and you can have it right here and not even move out of the chair."

Her eyes waited on him for an answer, a smile, a little nod, but he made no sign.

"Anyway," she went on, "I'll get you some cheese and crackers first."

"I don't want it," he said.

170

She moved uneasily in her chair, the large eyes still watching his face. "But you *must* have supper. I can easily do it here. I'd like to do it. We can have lamb chops. Or pork. Anything you want. Everything's in the freezer."

"Forget it," he said.

"But, darling, you *must* eat! I'll fix it anyway, and then you can have it or not, as you like."

She stood up and placed her sewing on the table by the lamp.

"Sit down," he said. "Just for a minute, sit down."

It wasn't till then that she began to get frightened.

"Go on," he said. "Sit down."

She lowered herself back slowly into the chair, watching him all the time with those large, bewildered eyes. He had finished the second drink and was staring down into the glass frowning.

"Listen," he said, "I've got something to tell you."

"What is it, darling? What's the matter?"

He had become absolutely motionless, and he kept his head down so that the light from the lamp beside him fell across the upper part of his face, leaving the chin and mouth in shadow. She noticed there was a little muscle moving near the corner of his left eye.

"This is going to be a bit of a shock to you, I'm afraid," he said. "But I've thought about it a good deal and I've decided the only thing to do is tell you right away. I hope you won't blame me too much."

And he told her. It didn't take long, four or five minutes at most, and she sat very still through it all, watching him with a kind of dazed horror as he went further and further away from her with each word.

"So there it is," he added. "And I know it's kind of a bad time to be telling you, but there simply wasn't any other way. Of course I'll give you money and see you're looked after. But there needn't really be any fuss. I hope not anyway. It wouldn't be very good for my job."

Her first instinct was not to believe any of it, to reject it all. It occurred to her that perhaps he hadn't even spoken, that she herself had imagined the whole thing. Maybe, if she went about her business and acted as though she hadn't been listening, then later, when she sort of woke up again, she might find none of it had ever happened.

"I'll get the supper," she managed to whisper, and this time he didn't stop her.

When she walked across the room she couldn't feel her feet touching the floor. She couldn't feel anything at all — except a slight nausea and a desire to vomit. Everything was automatic now — down the stairs to the cellar, the light switch, the deep freeze, the hand inside the cabinet taking hold of the first object it met. She lifted it out, and looked at it. It was wrapped in paper, so she took off the paper and looked at it again.

A leg of lamb.

All right then, they would have lamb for supper. She carried it upstairs, holding the thin bone-end of it with both her hands, and as she went through the living-room, she saw him standing over by the window with his back to her, and she stopped.

172

"For God's sake," he said, hearing her, but not turning round. "Don't make supper for me. I'm going out."

At that point, Mary Maloney simply walked up behind him and without any pause she swung the big frozen leg of lamb high in the air and brought it down as hard as she could on the back of his head.

She might just as well have hit him with a steel club.

She stepped back a pace, waiting, and the funny thing was that he remained standing there for at least four or five seconds, gently swaying. Then he crashed to the carpet.

The violence of the crash, the noise, the small table overturning, helped bring her out of the shock. She came out slowly, feeling cold and surprised, and she stood for a while blinking at the body, still holding the ridiculous piece of meat tight with both hands.

All right, she told herself. So I've killed him.

It was extraordinary, now, how clear her mind became all of a sudden. She began thinking very fast. As the wife of a detective, she knew quite well what the penalty would be. That was fine. It made no difference to her. In fact, it would be a relief. On the other hand, what about the child? What were the laws about murderers with unborn children? Did they kill them both — mother and child? Or did they wait until the tenth month? What did they do?

Mary Maloney didn't know. And she certainly wasn't prepared to take a chance.

She carried the meat into the kitchen, placed it in a pan, turned the oven on high, and shoved it inside. Then she washed her hands and ran upstairs to the bedroom. She sat down before the mirror, tidied her face, touched up her lips and face. She tried a smile. It came out rather peculiar. She tried again.

"Hullo Sam," she said brightly, aloud.

The voice sounded peculiar too.

"I want some potatoes please, Sam. Yes, and I think a can of peas."

That was better. Both the smile and the voice were coming out better now. She rehearsed it several times more. Then she ran downstairs, took her coat, went out the back door, down the garden, into the street.

It wasn't six o'clock yet and the lights were still on in the grocery shop.

"Hullo Sam," she said brightly, smiling at the man behind the counter.

"Why, good evening, Mrs Maloney. How're *you*?"

"I want some potatoes please, Sam. Yes, and I think a can of peas."

The man turned and reached up behind him on the shelf for the peas.

"Patrick's decided he's tired and doesn't want to eat out tonight," she told him. "We usually go out Thursdays, you know, and now he's caught me without any vegetables in the house."

"Then how about meat, Mrs Maloney?"

"No, I've got meat, thanks. I got a nice leg of lamb, from the freezer."

"Oh."

"I don't much like cooking it frozen, Sam, but I'm taking

a chance on it this time. You think it'll be all right?"

"Personally," the grocer said, "I don't believe it makes any difference. You want these Idaho potatoes?"

"Oh yes, that'll be fine. Two of those."

"Anything else?" The grocer cocked his head on one side, looking at her pleasantly. "How about afterwards? What you going to give him for afterwards?"

"Well – what would you suggest, Sam?"

The man glanced around his shop. "How about a nice big slice of cheesecake? I know he likes that."

"Perfect," she said. "He loves it."

And when it was all wrapped and she had paid she put on her brightest smile and said, "Thank you, Sam. Good night."

"Good night, Mrs Maloney. And thank *you*."

And now, she told herself as she hurried back, all she was doing now, she was returning home to her husband and he was waiting for his supper; and she must cook it good, and make it as tasty as possible because the poor man was tired; and if, when she entered the house, she happened to find anything unusual, or tragic, or terrible, then naturally it would be a shock and she'd become frantic with grief and horror. Mind you, she wasn't *expecting* to find anything. She was just going home with the vegetables. Mrs Patrick Maloney going home with the vegetables on Thursday evening to cook supper for her husband.

That's the way, she told herself. Do everything right and natural. Keep things absolutely natural and there'll be no need for any acting at all.

Therefore, when she entered the kitchen by the back

door, she was humming a little tune to herself and smiling.

"Patrick!" she called. "How are you darling?"

She put the parcel down on the table and went through into the living-room, and when she saw him lying there on the floor with his legs doubled up and one arm twisted back underneath his body, it really was rather a shock. All the old love and longing for him welled up inside her, and she ran over to him, knelt down beside him, and began to cry her heart out. It was easy. No acting was necessary.

A few minutes later she got up and went to the phone. She knew the number of the police station, and when the man at the other end answered, she cried to him, "Quick! Come quick! Patrick's dead!"

"Who's speaking?"

"Mrs Maloney. Mrs Patrick Maloney."

"You mean Patrick Maloney's dead?"

"I think so," she sobbed. "He's lying on the floor and I think he's dead."

"Be right over," the man said.

The car came over quickly, and when she opened the front door, two policemen walked in. She knew them both – she knew nearly all the men at that precinct – and she fell right into Jack Noonan's arms, weeping hysterically. He put her gently into a chair, then went over to join the other one, who was called O'Malley, kneeling by the body.

"Is he dead?" she cried.

"I'm afraid he is. What happened?"

Briefly, she told her story about going out to the grocer and coming back to find him on the floor. While she was talking, crying and talking, Noonan discovered a small patch of congealed blood on the dead man's head. He showed it to O'Malley who got up at once and hurried to the phone.

Soon, other men began to come into the house. First a doctor, then two detectives, one of whom she knew by name. Later, a police photographer arrived and took pictures, and a man who knew about fingerprints. There was a great deal of whispering and muttering beside the corpse, and the detectives kept asking her a lot of questions. But they always treated her kindly. She told her story again, this time right from the beginning, when Patrick had come in, and she was sewing, and he was tired, so tired he hadn't wanted to go out for supper. She told how she'd put the meat in the oven – "it's there now, cooking" – and how she'd slipped out to the grocer for vegetables, and come back to find him lying on the floor.

"Which grocer?" one of the detectives asked.

She told him, and he turned and whispered something to the other detective who immediately went outside into the street.

In fifteen minutes he was back with a page of notes, and there was more whispering, and through her sobbing she heard a few of the whispered phrases – "...acted quite normal ... very cheerful ... wanted to give him a good supper ... peas ... cheesecake ... impossible that she..."

After a while, the photographer and the doctor departed and two other men came in and took the corpse away on a stretcher. Then the fingerprint man went away. The two detectives remained, and so did the two policemen. They were exceptionally nice to her, and Jack Noonan asked if she wouldn't rather go somewhere else, to her sister's house perhaps, or to his own wife who would take care of her and put her up for the night.

No, she said. She didn't feel she could move even a yard at the moment. Would they mind awfully if she stayed just where she was until she felt better? She didn't feel too good at the moment, she really didn't.

Then hadn't she better lie down on the bed? Jack Noonan asked.

No, she said, she'd like to stay right where she was, in this chair. A little later perhaps, when she felt better, she would move.

So they left her there while they went about their business, searching the house. Occasionally one of the detectives asked her another question. Sometimes Jack Noonan spoke to her gently as he passed by. Her husband, he told her, had been killed by a blow on the back of the head administered with a heavy blunt instrument, almost certainly a large piece of metal. They were looking for the weapon. The murderer may have taken it with him, but on the other hand he may've thrown it away or hidden it somewhere on the premises.

"It's the old story," he said. "Get the weapon, and you've got the man."

Later, one of the detectives came up and sat beside her. Did she know, he asked, of anything in the house that could've been used as the weapon? Would she mind having a look around to see if anything was missing – a very big spanner for example, or a heavy metal vase.

They didn't have any heavy metal vases, she said.

"Or a big spanner?"

She didn't think they had a big spanner. But there might be some things like that in the garage.

The search went on. She knew that there were other policemen in the garden all around the house. She could hear their footsteps on the gravel outside, and sometimes she saw the flash of a torch through a chink in the curtains. It began to get late, nearly nine she noticed by the clock on the mantel. The four men searching the rooms seemed to be growing weary, a trifle exasperated.

"Jack," she said, the next time Sergeant Noonan went by. "Would you mind giving me a drink?"

"Sure I'll give you a drink. You mean this whisky?"

"Yes, please. But just a small one. It might make me feel better."

He handed her the glass.

"Why don't you have one yourself," she said. "You must be awfully tired. Please do. You've been very good to me."

"Well," he answered. "It's not strictly allowed, but I might take just a drop to keep me going."

One by one the others came in and were persuaded to take a little nip of whisky. They stood around rather awkwardly with the drinks in their hands, uncomfortable in her presence, trying to say consoling things to her. Sergeant Noonan wandered into the kitchen, came out quickly and said, "Look, Mrs Maloney. You know that oven of yours is still on, and the meat still inside."

"Oh *dear* me!" she cried. "So it is!"

"I better turn it off for you, hadn't I?"

"Will you do that, Jack. Thank you so much."

When the sergeant returned the second time, she looked at him with her large, dark, tearful eyes. "Jack Noonan," she said.

"Yes?"

"Would you do me a small favour – you and these others?"

"We can try, Mrs Maloney."

"Well," she said. "Here you all are, and good friends of dear Patrick's too, and helping to catch the man who killed him. You must be terribly hungry by now because it's long past your supper time, and I know Patrick would never forgive me, God bless his soul, if I allowed you to remain in his house without offering you decent hospitality. Why don't you eat up that lamb that's in the oven? It'll be cooked just right by now."

"Wouldn't dream of it," Sergeant Noonan said.

"Please," she begged. "Please eat it. Personally I couldn't touch a thing, certainly not what's been in the house when he was here. But it's all right for you. It'd be a favour to me if you'd eat it up. Then you can go on with your work again afterwards."

There was a good deal of hesitating among the four policemen, but they were clearly hungry, and in the end they were persuaded to go into the kitchen and help themselves. The woman stayed where she was, listening to them through the open door, and she could hear them speaking among themselves, their voices thick and sloppy because their mouths were full of meat.

"Have some more, Charlie?"

"No. Better not finish it."

"She *wants* us to finish it. She said so. Be doing her a favour."

"Okay then. Give me some more."

"That's the hell of a big club the guy must've used to hit poor Patrick," one of them was saying. "The doc says his skull was smashed all to pieces just like from a sledge-hammer."

"That's why it ought to be easy to find."

"Exactly what I say."

"Whoever done it, they're not going to be carrying a thing like that around with them longer than they need."

One of them belched.

"Personally, I think it's right here on the premises."

"Probably right under our very noses. What you think, Jack?"

And in the other room, Mary Maloney began to giggle.

Sredni Vashtar

Saki

Conradin was ten years old, and the doctor had pronounced his professional opinion that the boy would not live
another five years. The doctor was silky and effete, and
counted for little, but his opinion was endorsed by Mrs De
Ropp, who counted for nearly everything. Mrs De Ropp was
Conradin's cousin and guardian, and in his eyes she repre-
sented those three-fifths of the world that are necessary and
disagreeable and real; the other two-fifths, in perpetual
antagonism to the foregoing, were summed up in himself and
his imagination. One of these days Conradin supposed he
would succumb to the mastering pressure of wearisome
necessary things – such as illness and coddling restrictions
and drawn-out dullness. Without his imagination, which
was rampant under the spur of loneliness, he would have
succumbed long ago.

Mrs De Ropp would never, in her honestest moments,
have confessed to herself that she disliked Conradin, though
she might have been dimly aware that thwarting him "for his
good" was a duty which she did not find particularly irksome.
Conradin hated her with a desperate sincerity which he was
perfectly able to mask. Such few pleasures as he could con-
trive for himself gained an added relish from the likelihood

that they would be displeasing to his guardian, and from the realm of his imagination she was locked out – an unclean thing, which should find no entrance.

In the dull, cheerless garden, overlooked by so many windows that were ready to open with a message not to do this or that, or a reminder that medicines were due, he found little attraction. The few fruit-trees that it contained were set jealously apart from his plucking, as though they were rare specimens of their kind blooming in an arid waste; it would probably have been difficult to find a market-gardener who would have offered ten shillings for the entire yearly produce. In a forgotten corner, however, almost hidden behind a dismal shrubbery, was a disused tool-shed of respectable proportions, and within its walls Conradin found a haven, something that took on the varying aspects of a playroom and a cathedral. He had peopled it with a legion of familiar phantoms, evoked partly from fragments of history and partly from his own brain, but it also boasted two inmates of flesh and blood. In one corner lived a ragged-plumaged Houdan hen, on which the boy lavished an affection that had scarcely another outlet. Further back in the gloom stood a large hutch, divided into two compartments, one of which was fronted with close iron bars. This was the abode of a large polecat ferret, which a friendly butcher-boy had once smuggled, cage and all, into its present quarters, in exchange for a long-secreted hoard of small silver. Conradin was dreadfully afraid of the lithe, sharp-fanged beast, but it was his most treasured possession. Its very presence in the tool-shed was a secret and fearful joy, to be kept scrupulously from the knowledge of the Woman, as he privately dubbed his cousin. And one day, out of heaven knows what material, he spun the beast a wonderful name, and from that moment it grew into a god and a religion. The Woman indulged in religion once a week at a church near by, and took Conradin with her, but to him the church service was an alien rite in the House of Rimmon. Every Thursday, in the dim and musty silence of the tool-shed, he worshipped with mystic and elaborate ceremonial before the wooden hutch where dwelt Sredni Vashtar, the great ferret. Red flowers in their season and scarlet berries in the winter-time were offered at his shrine, for he was a god who laid some special stress on the fierce impatient side of things, as opposed to the Woman's religion, which, as far as Conradin could observe, went to great lengths in the contrary direction. And on great festivals powdered nutmeg was strewn in front of his hutch, an important feature of the offering being that the nutmeg had to be stolen. These festivals were of irregular occurrence, and were chiefly appointed to celebrate some passing event. On one occasion, when Mrs De Ropp suffered from acute toothache for three days, Conradin kept up the festival during the entire three days, and almost succeeded in persuading himself that Sredni Vashtar was personally responsible for the toothache. If the malady had lasted for another day the supply of nutmeg would have given out.

The Houdan hen was never drawn into the cult of Sredni Vashtar. Conradin had long ago settled that she was an Anabaptist. He did not pretend to have the remotest knowledge as to what an Anabaptist was, but he privately hoped that it was dashing and not very respectable. Mrs De Ropp was the ground plan on which he based and detested all respectability.

After a while Conradin's absorption in the tool-shed began to attract the notice of his guardian. "It is not good for him to be pottering down there in all weathers," she promptly decided, and at breakfast one morning she announced that the Houdan hen had been sold and taken away overnight. With her short-sighted eyes she peered at Conradin, waiting for an outbreak of rage and sorrow, which she was ready to rebuke with a flow of excellent precepts and reasoning. But Conradin said nothing: there was nothing to be said. Something perhaps in his white set face gave her a momentary qualm, for at tea that afternoon there was toast on the table, a delicacy which she usually banned on the ground that it was bad for him; also because the making of it "gave trouble", a deadly offence in the middle-class feminine eye.

"I thought you liked toast," she exclaimed with an injured air, observing that he did not touch it.

"Sometimes," said Conradin.

In the shed that evening there was an innovation in the worship of the hutch-god. Conradin had been wont to chant his praises; tonight he asked a boon.

"Do one thing for me, Sredni Vashtar."

The thing was not specified. As Sredni Vashtar was a god he must be supposed to know. And, choking back a sob as he looked at the other empty corner, Conradin went back to the world he so hated.

And every night, in the welcome darkness of his bedroom, and every evening in the dusk of the tool-shed, Conradin's bitter litany went up: "Do one thing for me, Sredni Vashtar."

Mrs De Ropp noticed that the visits to the shed did not cease, and one day she made a further journey of inspection.

"What are you keeping in that locked hutch?" she asked. "I believe it's guinea-pigs. I'll have them all cleared away."

Conradin shut his lips tight, but the Woman ransacked his bedroom till she found the carefully hidden key, and forthwith marched down to the shed to complete her discovery. It was a cold afternoon, and Conradin had been bidden to keep to the house. From the furthest window of the dining-room the door of the shed could just be seen beyond the corner of the shrubbery, and there Conradin stationed himself. He saw the Woman enter, and then he imagined her opening the door of the sacred hutch and peering down with her short-sighted eyes into the thick straw bed where his god lay hidden. Perhaps she would prod at the straw in her clumsy impatience. And Conradin fervently breathed his prayer for the last time. But he knew as he prayed that he did not believe. He knew that the Woman would come out presently with that pursed smile he loathed so well on her face, and that in an hour or two the gardener would carry away his wonderful god, a god no longer, but a simple brown ferret in a hutch. And he knew that the Woman would triumph always as she triumphed now, and that he would grow ever more sickly under her pestering and domineering, and superior wisdom, till one day nothing would matter much more with him, and the doctor would be proved right. And in the sting and misery of his defeat, he began to chant loudly and defiantly the hymn of his threatened idol:

Sredni Vashtar went forth,
His thoughts were red thoughts and his teeth were white.
His enemies called for peace, but he brought them death.
Sredni Vashtar the Beautiful.

And then of a sudden he stopped his chanting and drew closer to the window-pane. The door of the shed still stood ajar as it had been left, and the minutes were slipping by. They were long minutes, but they slipped by nevertheless. He watched the starlings running and flying in little parties across the lawn; he counted them over and over again, with one eye always on that swinging door. A sour-faced maid came in to lay the table for tea, and still Conradin stood and waited and watched. Hope had crept by inches into his heart, and now a look of triumph began to blaze in his eyes that had only known the wistful patience of defeat. Under his breath, with a furtive exultation, he began once again the paean of victory and devastation. And presently his eyes were rewarded: out through that doorway came a long, low, yellow and brown beast, with eyes a-blink at the waning daylight, and dark wet stains around the fur of jaw and throat. Conradin dropped on his knees. The great polecat ferret made its way down to a small brook at the foot of the garden, drank for a moment, then crossed a little plank bridge and was lost to sight in the bushes. Such was the passing of Sredni Vashtar.

"Tea is ready," said the sour-faced maid; "where is the mistress?"

"She went down to the shed some time ago," said Conradin.

And while the maid went to summon her mistress to tea, Conradin fished a toasting-fork out of the sideboard drawer and proceeded to toast himself a piece of bread. And during the toasting of it and the buttering of it with much butter and the slow enjoyment of eating it, Conradin listened to the noises and silences which fell in quick spasms beyond the dining-room door. The loud foolish screaming of the maid, the answering chorus of wondering ejaculations from the kitchen region, the scuttering footsteps and hurried embassies for outside help, and then, after a lull, the scared sobbings and the shuffling tread of those who bore a heavy burden into the house.

"Whoever will break it to the poor child? I couldn't for the life of me!" exclaimed a shrill voice. And while they debated the matter among themselves, Conradin made himself another piece of toast.

About the Authors

ART BUCHWALD (1925–) One of America's great political humorists and columnists. Born in New York during the Depression, Buchwald first became involved with journalism whilst living in France and writing for the *Paris Herald Tribune*. His column became extremely popular and he travelled extensively before returning to live in Washington. Buchwald won a Pulitzer Prize in 1982 and is the author of thirty books. His political satire column is syndicated in hundreds of newspapers around the world.

IVAN (ALEKSEYEVICH) BUNIN (1870–1953) Russian poet, short-story writer, novelist and translator. Bunin is best known for his writing about the decay of the Russian nobility and his realistic depictions of village life. He was awarded the Pushkin Poetry Prize in 1901, and in 1933 became the first Russian to win the Nobel Prize for Literature. Amongst his works are *Derevnya* (1910, *The Village*), "Gospodin iz San-Francisco" (1916, "The Gentleman from San Francisco") and *Vospominaniya* (1950, *Memories and Portraits*).

ROALD DAHL (1916–90) Welsh-born writer of short stories and stories for children. Dahl was posted to Washington after being injured as a pilot in World War II and it was here that he started his writing career. His collections for adults include *Over to You* (1946), *Someone Like You* (1953) and *Kiss Kiss* (1959). Many of these stories were televised in the series *Tales of the Unexpected*. Amongst his most popular works for children are *James and the Giant Peach* (1961), *Charlie and the Chocolate Factory* (1964), *The BFG* (1982) and *Matilda* (1988).

GRAHAM GREENE (1904–91) English novelist, short-story writer and playwright. Greene was educated at Balliol College, Oxford. He worked on *The Times* and *The Spectator*, becoming literary editor of the latter in 1940. Amongst his greatest novels are *Brighton Rock* (1938), *The Power and the Glory* (1940), *The Heart of the Matter* (1948) and *The End of the Affair* (1951). His work also includes *Twenty-One Stories* (1954) and plays such as *The Living Room* (1953), *The Potting Shed* (1958) and *The Complaisant Lover* (1959).

VLADIMIR (GALAKTIONOVICH) KOROLENKO (1853–1921) Russian short-story writer and journalist. Born in the Ukraine, Korolenko was exiled to Siberia in 1879 for his revolutionary activities. He was released after six years, at which time his best-known story was published, *Son makara* (1885, *Makar's Dream*). He was editor of the review *Russkoe Bogatstvo*, supporting young writers such as Maksim Gorky. He retired to the Ukraine after the October Revolution in 1917 where he wrote his unfinished autobiography *Istoriya moyego sovremennika* (1910–21, *The History of My Contemporary*).

D(AVID) H(ERBERT) LAWRENCE (1885–1930) British novelist, poet, essayist and short-story writer. His intense writing is full of psychological insight and is frequently concerned with man's alienation in modern industrial society, often regarding nature and instinct as a contrast and a cure. His works include the novels *Sons and Lovers* (1913), *The Rainbow* (1915), *Women in Love* (1920) and *Lady Chatterley's Lover* (1928), and the short stories *The Captain's Doll* (1923) and *The Fox* (1923).

STEPHEN (BUTLER) LEACOCK (1869–1944) Canadian humorist, lecturer and author. Born in England, Stephen Leacock immigrated to Canada with his family at the age of six. He went to university, then taught at colleges and universities until his retirement in 1936. His work includes many publications on history and political economy, but he was renowned for his humour both in and out of lectures, including the works *Literary Lapses* (1910), *Nonsense Novels* (1911) and *Frenzied Fiction* (1918).

JACK LONDON (1876–1916) (John Griffith London) American novelist and short-story writer. Born in San Francisco, London grew up in poverty and used reading as a form of escapism. In 1897 he joined the gold rush to the Klondike, returning with ideas that inspired his future writing. He became the highest-paid writer in the world but financial difficulties led to him drinking heavily and he committed suicide at the age of forty. His works include *The Call of the Wild* (1903), *The Sea-Wolf* (1904) and *White Fang* (1906).

GUY DE MAUPASSANT (1850–93) French novelist, poet and short-story writer. A pupil of Gustave Flaubert and a contemporary of Émile Zola and Henry James, Maupassant's mastery of the writer's craft – including his perceptive observations and precise style – led him to be widely regarded as France's greatest short-story writer. His works include the novels *Une Vie* (1883), *Bel-Ami* (1885) and *Pierre et Jean* (1888), and the short stories "Boule de suif" (1880), "Le Parapluie" (1884), "Les Soeurs Rondoli" (1884), "Une Famille" (1886) and "Le Rendez-vous" (1889).

MARINA MIZZAU Italian university professor and writer. Mizzau is a professor of psychology at the University of Bologna. She is interested in the psychology of linguistics and communication and has written many papers on the subject. This interest is also evident in her fiction: often focusing on one small episode in everyday life, Mizzau's stories investigate the relationship of language to its context, and also to the hearer and speaker. Her fiction includes *Come i delfini* (1988) and *I bambini non volano* (1992).

EDGAR ALLAN POE (1809–49) American poet, literary critic and short-story writer. Born in Boston and orphaned at an early age, Poe was brought up by his godfather, John Allan. He was respected as a literary critic and editor, and was influential in turning short-story writing into an art form. His work includes "The Fall of the House of Usher" (1839), *Tales of the Grotesque and Arabesque* (1840), "The Pit and the Pendulum" (1842) and "The Murders in the Rue Morgue" (1841), a significant predecessor of the modern-day detective novel.

SAKI (1870–1916) (Hector Hugh Munro) Scottish satirist and author. Born in Burma, Saki was sent to live with his aunts in England at the age of two. He found them to be strict and unsympathetic, and this episode influenced his later writing, including the short story "Sredni Vashtar". Saki was educated in England, then worked as a journalist and novelist. His works include *Reginald* (1904), *Reginald in Russia* (1910), *The Chronicles of Clovis* (1911) and *Beasts and Super-Beasts* (1914). Saki was killed in action in World War I.

JAMES (GROVER) THURBER (1894–1961) American writer and cartoonist. Thurber had several newspaper jobs before joining *The New Yorker*. He mainly considered himself a writer, but his drawing was first published in this magazine in 1931, and his stock characters have since become legendary. Thurber's works include *Is Sex Necessary?* (1929, co-author E B White), *My Life and Hard Times* (1933) and "The Secret Life of Walter Mitty" (1942), as well as the children's works *The 13 Clocks* (1950) and *The Wonderful O* (1957).

P(ELHAM) G(RENVILLE) WODEHOUSE (1881–1975) English journalist, story writer and humorist. Wodehouse lived in the UK, the USA and France during his life. He wrote newspaper and magazine articles, and worked on many musical shows in the USA. He is best known for his comic writing about eccentric English upper-class characters, including *Leave It to Psmith* (1923), *The Inimitable Jeeves* (1924), *Young Men in Spats* (1936), *Code of the Woosters* (1938) and *Bertie Sees It Through* (1955). Wodehouse was knighted in 1975 shortly before his death.